THE CREED

Brother Robertson
God bless you!

Frank C. Davis

8/98

FRANK C. DAVIS

The Creed
ISBN 1-880536-11-0
Copyright © 1998 by
Frank C. Davis

Published by
Daily Word Publishing
P. O. Box 1448
Live Oak, Florida 32064

DEDICATION

This book is lovingly dedicated to my four children: Laura, Leslie, Frank, and Lisa, whom I love very much.

1

"Mr. Watson?" the female voice blurted over the intercom.

Jerry Watson did not seem to notice the call and slumped further in his Comfortzone executive chair, his right elbow rested on the rich leather arm and his hand gently cradled his chin. He placed the toe portion of his brown Bally shoe on the elegant mahogany desk and eased the chair back slightly and stared out the spacious window of his 40th floor office at the Peachtree Center. He looked over the skyline of the city of Atlanta at the huge dome of Stone Mountain in the distance–a chunk of granite defended by a ragged but determined band of Confederates during the Civil War. It had since become a major tourist attraction with the South's most magnificent laser light show. It was an awesome view by anyone's standards. "Jerry, you have the best darned view in the city of Atlanta," a fellow attorney once observed.

"Mr. Watson?" the voice inquired again.

Jerry ignored the interruption again as he peered out the window at the giant, immovable rock. The sight of the resolute and unconquerable image contrasted starkly with his present situation. He felt as if he were in quicksand and sinking fast. He had come far–very far–from the little town of Washburn in south Georgia where he started out more than forty years before. He had struggled as a troubled youth to find direction, but now he was a famous international lawyer, and an advisor to the

President of the United States.

His lofty position sounded impressive, it opened a lot of doors and gave Jerry opportunities he would not have had otherwise, but at the moment he did not feel very significant or important. He plummeted to a depth of despair he had never experienced while waves of dark clouds hovered over him. He gazed out the window much too often and he was not eating very well, sleep escaped him. For the first time in his life he actually thought about what it would be like to end his life. His wife, Mary Ann, worried about his not getting enough sleep and losing too much weight the last several weeks.

The last several weeks! The last several weeks had been nightmarish. What had started out as a dream a little over three years ago had changed so dramatically in *the last several weeks*. In all his 20 years of practicing law and public service he had never suffered such venomous personal attacks. Not only had his President come under hostile fire but Jerry himself was under intense scrutiny by the media. He was castigated by political opponents, and considered suspect by some of the President's own staff. His confidence was badly shaken. He was hurt, angry, and frustrated and fear gnawed in his belly. What went wrong? Jerry tried, once again, to put things into perspective–to reason out how things had reached this point.

"Mr. Watson?" the voice called again.

"Uh, yes, Mrs. Reed." Jerry wheeled around in his luxury chair to face his desk. Jerry's wide mahogany desk was unusually clean for an important man like him. There only a day planner, his phone, a yellow legal pad, one blue file, and a clear paper weight in the shape of a diamond with a traditional twenty dollar gold piece in the

2

middle. Jerry had long ago adopted a policy of working on only one thing at a time and he kept his desk free of other distracting materials. He worked more effectively and productively when his desk was uncluttered, and it made him feel more in control.

"Mr. Watson! Mr. O'Grady is on line three." "Thank you Mrs. Reed." Jerry reached over, picked up the phone and pressed line three. "Hello Casey."

"Hello Jerry, how is it going?" Casey was a writer for the Atlanta Journal and a good friend and confidant. A Bostonian, he had been writing editorials for the past twenty five years and was an institution in Atlanta and the state of Georgia. All the political big wigs paid him homage and it was very difficult to get elected if you got on his bad side. Even though he was an old line liberal, because of his fairness, he carried a lot of political clout even with conservatives. He called things as he saw them, no matter whom or what he was writing about. He and Jerry became fast friends just after Jerry and his family moved to Atlanta in the seventies. They met at an Atlanta Braves–Pittsburgh Pirates game and shared a spot together under the stands at Atlanta-Fulton County Stadium while outlasting a fifth inning thunderstorm. They began talking and discovered they both enjoyed politics. And although Jerry was staunchly conservative and Casey was liberal, they seemed to share much in common. They both had a desire to help others and work to make America great. Over the years Casey consulted Jerry on the conservative point of view and Jerry would seek Casey's advice on matters to which he thought his party should be more attuned such as civil rights and the environment. Although they held widely different views on many subjects, they respected and trusted each other.

"What's up Casey? Do you need a quote from an unnamed source close to the Administration?" Jerry joked, he tried to sound like himself.

"No. I've done laid that baby to rest. I'm calling with some information I feel you need to know."

"What's that?"

"I was talking with Dale Reeves, an old friend of mine at CNN here in Atlanta. He told me, confidentially of course, that Sue Freeman of Townsend, Short, and Dauper, your friendly competitor for international trade clients, found out by coincidence that you may have something in your past that could be very embarrassing to you and the administration. She phoned a buddy at CNN and thought he might like to do a human interest story on one of the President's advisors. Of course it's a subterfuge, they're gonna sandbag you Jerry and put you on the spot while the camera rolls."

"She what?" Jerry gasped. "What are you talking about Casey? What is she supposed to know about my past, and who told her?"

"Hey! Take it easy," Casey cautioned. "I'm not the enemy. I'm just delivering a message that I thought you should know. I don't want to see you get blind sided. You know I don't go for that kind of tactic. Those TV news guys are always looking for something inflammatory to cover, especially when it concerns a celebrity or politician."

"Well, I'm neither one," Jerry retorted.

"I know you're not. But you do advise the most powerful man in the world."

Sweat popped out on Jerry's brow and he wiped it with the back of his hand, he loosened his tie and shifted uneasily in his chair. "Don't remind me," he insisted.

"The CNN Reporter is Adrian Phillips and he's going to be contacting you by this weekend. Don't be surprised if you see a camera crew outside your office soon. Jerry, I believe they're up to no good. I'd watch them."

"Thanks for being a friend Casey." Jerry knew the elderly gentleman could use information about his past and humiliate him with it, and who could blame him? His ideological friends were breathing fire on the neck of the president, and they desperately wanted to win the upcoming presidential election. It was a great opportunity for him to further embarrass the President, but Jerry knew Casey was a man of integrity and would not do it.

"Jerry," Casey said softly. "You know I could squeeze you real hard on this, but I won't. I don't care about your past, you've proved to me that you're an honest man. However, if there is something to this rabbit trail, then I'm gonna be in the hunt just like everybody else, but I promise I'll be fair with you."

There was a click on the other end and Jerry replaced the receiver in the cradle. White hot fear seared his whole body, a sick feeling rose from his stomach, an acid taste filled his mouth. "My God! What am I going to do?" he blurted out to an empty office.

The improbable situation in which Jerry now found himself did not happen over night, but began as a series of events which took place over several months. The challenger, Kenneth W. Morton, was elected president in an upset victory over the incumbent in the last election. To everyone's surprise the major issue of the campaign was the U. S. trade deficit. Exports were down and imports were up which produced the worst trade imbalance in U. S. history. Contrary to what the experts predicted, the North American Free Trade Agreement, did not fuel the economy but did in fact force many jobs south. It did not help matters that competition from countries in the Pacific rim put additional pressure on the economy and as a result unemployment soared, industrial and textile production dropped and people became desperate. The economy was the top priority with the voters and even U. S. troops in Eastern Europe protecting a fragile truce could not displace it as the number one issue of the campaign. The American people were looking for relief and Kenneth Morton offered a workable and practical solution to the problem. He talked tough. He would propose and support legislation to repeal NAFTA, he would immediately impose trade tariffs on the most popular Japanese products; and he would forge new partnerships with developing countries which had money to spend. His tough stand attracted a number of high profile politicians, businessmen and leaders who not only endorsed his economic plan, but threw their support behind him.

Jerry had been a major player in putting together the strategy that propelled Morton's campaign to the cutting edge of economic issues. He was a strategist on foreign affairs concerning trade and an expert in Asian affairs. His education and experience had prepared him well to serve in that capacity. He had majored in Political Science and Economics at the University of Georgia and received his law degree from Duke University Law School. He had also spent one year in Japan as an exchange student and while there he developed a desire to pursue a career in international law, specifically in the area of international trade. He had become a top negotiator in a number of trade wars and his stock rose when he facilitated a mega-merger between U. S. Kodak and Japanese Fuji. When Kenneth Morton assembled his economic campaign advisors, Jerry headed the list.

The president-elect and his staff were on top of the world for several months and a euphoria swept the country as he made several high profile speeches outlining his vision for America. His popularity grew despite attempts by opponents to derail his proposals, harass his appointments and assassinate his character. And although he had to work with a Congress controlled by his political opponents, he pushed through many programs on his popularity alone. But after two years things slowed down and grid-lock set in. The indecisiveness by both the President and Congress on major trade issues and the economy, not to mention social issues such as the divisive abortion question, had a negative impact on the public consciousness and the country became restless. The American public looked for someone to blame and the *Inside the Beltway* crowd made President Morton the scapegoat.

The country settled into a malaise, Consumer confidence plummeted, the stock market dropped, and interest rates rose. At a strategy meeting with the President and the Secretary of Commerce, Jerry suggested the President make a series of high profile economic decisions including the lifting of the trade embargo against Cuba. He pushed hard for this and persuasively argued that now was the time to take action on this matter as it would do three things: it would be seen as a symbol of his boldness to open new markets for American goods and thereby break the stalemate; it would show his willingness to break down any and all trade barriers and make the U. S. competitive in other countries; and it would demonstrate that the President was not interested in using trade as a weapon to punish the average citizen in other countries, many of whom struggle to survive.

The policy seemed sound, and polls suggested it was popular, but the President badly miscalculated the response from the anti-Castro community in the States. He was prepared for fierce political opposition but was shocked and dismayed when a radical fringe group hijacked a luxury liner leaving Miami for the Bahamas. It ended with 24 people killed when commandos raided the ship and freed the passengers. The media soundly trounced the President on his decision to lift the embargo and blamed him for not predicting such a response, and failing to provide adequate protection for American citizens. Consequently Jerry felt not only the rebuke of the President and his handlers, but also the sting of the media. He had not figured on being in the middle of a political fire storm and it plunged him into despair. He blamed himself for what happened. "I used to enjoy my work and life," he thought.

And for himself, Jerry feared the worst had not begun, for there was one bit of information no one knew about–except maybe Sue Freeman and the CNN reporter. No one knew about embarrassing events of Jerry's past, not even his wife Mary Ann. How could he tell anyone now? It would be red meat for every news reporter in America. He had tried to tell the FBI agents who interviewed him while he was under consideration as counselor to the President, but they hurriedly concluded their investigation and moved on to other matters. Before Jerry knew it, the investigation was all over, by then he felt it was too late.

What would another appointment debacle do to the President's reelection chances? He had witnessed the carnage left by the unveiling of descriptive pasts of two nominees for top administration posts. One was a CEO of a major corporation who was nominated for Secretary of the Interior who, it was revealed, had been convicted of shoplifting when he was seventeen. He was shamed right out of Washington and nearly lost his position because of a foolish act he committed nearly thirty years earlier. Then there was the highly qualified woman who was nominated for Attorney General who had had a stormy affair with a well known politician some twenty years earlier in the capital city. The media blew the story out of proportion and the President was forced to withdraw her name from nomination. And although Jerry did not command a Cabinet level position or other prestigious job in the Administration, he felt he was still a target and could prove to be an embarrassment to President Morton.

Jerry suddenly felt drained as he fell back in his leather chair. He put his foot on his desk and kicked away from it. Frustration ate at him. He was not used to having his life and every decision scrutinized in the national press. He pushed against a great weight to raise himself from the chair. He stood to his full six feet and trudged across the plush gray carpeting to the window which overlooked the busy street below. He looked down at the match box size cars that moved along the narrow street and thought, "What would it be like to jump out of this window?" He quickly pushed the thought from his mind.

"I've got to get in touch with my feelings," he thought.

He looked over in the corner of the spacious office and spied his private file drawer. He made his way over to the mahogany cabinet and bent over and opened the second drawer where he found the well worn leather briefcase he had used while in law school. When he had retrieved the case he closed the drawer, moved to the opposite side of the room and sat down in a visitor's arm chair. He carefully opened the briefcase that contained treasured mementos and keepsakes from his past–items that reminded him of where he had come from–things that brought him a mixture of joy and pain.

He reached in and pulled out a picture he had made for his mother when he was in first grade. It was constructed of crushed egg shells glued onto a shoe box lid. He fondly remembered how much fun he had had in first grade–the new friends, the games, his first reader with Dick, Jane and Spot. But then a grimness washed over his face when he remembered how things went steadily downhill and he dropped out of school and suffered failure.

He quickly moved on to a packet of yellowed sheets held together by a spindly rubber band–Jerry's grades from junior college. This was his first educational endeavor after he had taken and passed the exam for his General Equivalency Diploma. A quiet satisfaction filled him as he remembered–all A's. The next item that caught his attention was the acceptance letter from Duke University Law School. Jerry smiled, recalling the shock of his friends, "Jerry Watson is going to law school! That's impossible. He didn't even finish high school. How could he possibly make it?"

Jerry came to one of his favorite items—a musty green picture album with yellowed newspaper clippings. He smiled again when he skimmed the headlines and looked at the faded pictures of the football players—his favorite team, the World Champion Green Bay Packers. Bart Starr at quarterback, Jim Taylor and Paul Horning in the backfield and Jerry Kramer, the premier guard in the league. Ray Nitschke was as tough as they came at linebacker and of course the venerated Vince Lombardi was the best coach in the NFL.

He dug deeper into the side pocket of the briefcase and found two more items dear to him—a picture and a Barlow knife. The picture was of his sixth grade class, it was creased at the top but otherwise in good condition. There he was with his favorite teacher, Mrs. Richardson, one of the precious people from Jerry's painful past and the person who had more to do with his success than anyone else. She was beautiful. He thought about her gentleness, kindness, and love for her students. To the young boy who detested school and had to be coerced and threatened to attend, she had been the difference between success and failure. Her belief in him had had a profound effect on him later in his life. She instilled in him the principles upon which he had built his life and work. Jerry looked down at the Barlow knife, opened it, and to his delight there was enough of an edge to trim a hang nail on his ring finger. That done he folded the blade and placed the knife back in the pocket.

Finally he found the parchment for which he had been looking. It was rolled up and held together with a faded red ribbon. He gently untied the fragile ribbon and slowly unrolled the paper. At the top in big, bold letters was written, *This Certificate Given to Master Jerry Watson For*

Outstanding Achievement in Mrs. Richardson's Sixth Grade Class. It was inscribed with four principles of success: Have Faith in God; Get an Education; Work Hard; and Take Personal Responsibility for Your Actions. At the bottom it was dated and signed–Mrs. Margaret Richardson, Sixth Grade Teacher.

"The Creed, The Creed." Jerry half whispered and put his finger to his pursed lips. "Haven't I followed the principles? What went wrong? I thought if I upheld these laws I would be a success." Jerry pondered the principles for a moment then whispered the words from the parchment once more, "Have faith in God; Get an education; Work hard; and Take personal responsibility for your actions." What was missing?

As he replaced the items in the leather brief case he did not feel any better. He could not forget about the CNN reporter and the potential embarrassment to the president and to himself. Jerry was a very proud person and he did not believe he could stand to be humiliated any further. He was confused about what to do. He wavered, something he rarely did. He thought he would call the President's Chief of Staff, Nicole Jantzen, and tell her his dark secret. But he could not bring himself to do it. He was ashamed to confess his failures. He could be fired, or worse, he might be set upon by the vultures in and out of the administration who despised him.

He had to get away for a few days, to think, to plan, to decide what to do. He picked up the receiver and dialed his home number. After three rings a cheerful voice answered, "Hello."

"Hello honey," Jerry mustered a cheerful response. "How are things going today?" Mary Ann was the light of Jerry's life. Ever since he met her at Duke University she had been the only person with whom he wanted to spend his life. She always lifted him up when he was down and he could not think of one instance where she was not sensitive to his needs. As he became involved with the presidential campaign and subsequently as an advisor, she supplied the needed strength and perspective to help Jerry cope with the political and media pressure. And she was a very godly woman. She was faithful to her church and many times Jerry heard her praying throughout the night when times got tough for him or when one of the children was going through difficulties. But this time even her positive attitude and strong commitment to God did not seem to help Jerry.

"Do you really want to know dear?" Mary Ann said in her characteristic style. "Frank is over at John's house, they're building a tree house in Mr. Jackson's backyard. Do I have to remind you of how he responded last time the boys hammered nails in his prize Magnolia tree? Susan is in her room brooding because she's not old enough to go to the mall on her bike. And George, your favorite cat, is refusing to come out from under the bed once again. So how's your day going?"

"Wow, it sounds like you're having a tough day, honey."

"Oh Jerry, you know it's just the daily things of life. I don't have to face the kinds of pressures you do. I'm really blessed to have the wonderful husband and children I have. How are things at the office?"

"Everything is going well," Jerry lied.

"Now, Jerry! I can still detect that edge in your voice, and it sounds more strained. Has something else happened to add to your frustrations?"

Jerry wanted to unload it all on her, but he just could not do it. She was his cheerleader, the one person in all the world who supported him and believed in him completely. He did not want to do anything to make her worry.

"Not really, but you know the political climate is heating up every day and I can still feel it." Jerry was willing to tell her what she already knew. "But you're right, I'm still a little uptight and I thought I might take the next couple of days and drive over to that campground on the other side of Birmingham we went to about three years ago. You remember, the one just west and north of the city. I think it would help me to get away and think about everything, on my own. Do you mind?"

"Of course not." She seemed a bit offended that he would ask her permission. She had lived with him for twenty-five years and she completely trusted him. "Honey, you know you don't need my approval to do what you think is best, but you know I will miss you. I don't like for you to be away any more than you have to be, but you have to do what you have to do."

"I wonder sometimes if I did the right thing in accepting such an important role as advisor to the President."

"I have always thought it was the right thing, Jerry," she firmly stated. "I believe God placed you in the President's inner circle so you could help him and support him. You know how I feel about that."

Of course he knew that she was convinced God had opened the door for him to be part of President Morton's advisors. As an outspoken born again Christian, Morton was seen by Mary Ann and her Christian friends as God's man, and people like Jerry were divinely sent to hold up his arms as

Joshua and Hur had held up the arms of Moses.

"You know that all the lies and attacks against President Morton are spiritually inspired because he's a Christian, and specifically because he's pro-life. Honey, he needs you in his corner."

"Like you're in my corner?" Jerry smiled.

"Darling, you know I love you no matter what. I'll support you in any decision you make, even if you decide to leave his counsel."

"Thank you for that vote of confidence, Dear." Jerry knew he did not have the option of leaving, at least not now, it would raise too many questions. And besides, after the CNN interview he might not have the luxury of making that decision himself. Someone else would probably make it."

"I'll be home in a couple of hours to pack," Jerry said. "I love you," he added.

"I love you too."

There was a click on the other end and Jerry pressed the intercom. "Mrs. Reed, would you come in here with your pad please?"

Jerry's secretary entered his office with pad and pen in hand. She seated herself in front of his desk and looked up at the slightly graying man.

"Mrs. Reed, I'm going to be out of town for the next two days. I know that this is unexpected and that I have several very important appointments, but it is completely unavoidable so I'll need your help in rescheduling everything."

"Is everything okay Mr. Watson, I mean, is your family all right?"

"Yes, they're fine. It has nothing to do with them. I'll stay in touch with you and with the White House, of course."

"Yes sir."

2

Jerry quietly shut the kitchen door and stepped into the garage with a cup of fresh coffee in his hand. He walked over to his 1970 Ford F100 pick up truck and threw an overnight bag in the back. The shiny blue truck was immaculate—more than a collector's item—it was special to Jerry because it had belonged to his brother Dale. Dale had bought the truck in the fall of 1969 just before he went to Viet Nam. When he knew that he was going to ship out in 1970 he asked Jerry to take care of it while he was away.

"If anything happens to me, you can have it. I've got insurance so it will be paid for." Dale told him just before he stepped onto the Greyhound bus in Washburn that would take him to Fort Bragg, North Carolina and then to Viet Nam. Jerry never saw Dale alive again. He was killed in a fire fight with the Viet Cong in some little village with a name Jerry could not pronounce. After that, he could not bear to part with the truck. It was also the best vehicle he had ever owned, including some of the finest luxury automobiles money could buy. He did take a bit of ribbing from his associates when he drove it to work, though.

He checked the camping equipment he had put in the truck the night before. He ran his fingers over the nylon tent which would sleep three comfortably and made sure he had the bag with the stakes and poles. The Coleman stove and lantern were next to the cab. He had an assortment of

17

cooking utensils, a couple of fishing rods, and a machete which always came in handy on such trips. There was the container with water since Jerry anticipated staying where there would be no hookups. The last thing he checked was his chrome plated .38 pistol. Mary Ann had never liked having a hand gun in the house, especially when the kids were smaller, so Jerry kept it unloaded so an accident would not occur. However, he always carried it with him when he traveled away from home in his vehicle. He opened the chamber and made sure it had six rounds in it, spun it around once, snapped it back in place, and put it back in the holster. When he opened the driver's side door he heard the usual frantic scratching at the back door of the garage. He smiled and put the gun under the seat and headed for the door. He was not about to forget Blue, the most faithful and loyal canine companion in all the world. Blue was a mutt Jerry had found on one of the family camping trips in the North Carolina mountains five years earlier. The family immediately fell in love with the cute little brown puppy with the black eye.

Jerry opened the door and said, "Come on, boy."

Blue darted to the back of the truck and sat on his hind legs, tail wagging, and looked up at the truck in anticipation. Jerry moved to the rear of the truck and let down the tail gate and watched as the big dog jumped up and found his favorite spot near the back. He walked around in a circle a couple of times before he finally lay down.

Jerry closed the tail gate and walked to the driver's side, climbed up into the cab, put the key in the ignition and turned it over. The older model truck started easily and the engine purred with a low hum. Jerry put it in reverse and eased it out of the garage and onto Willow Lane which ran in front of his house. He glanced at his watch, it was 6:38 a. m. as he shifted into first gear and slowly pulled away from his home and family. He looked in the mirror at the lovely split level home he had lived in for the past twelve years until he rounded a curve and it was no longer in sight. A touch of sadness filled him, he was a family man and had never liked to leave home. Now that his oldest daughter, Alison, was 21 and away at Florida State University, there were eleven year old Frank and nine year old Susan still at home. It wasn't easy for him to leave because he did not know for sure where he was going and how long he would be gone. He knew he had to get some breathing room and some time to think. And whatever was to happen would happen.

Jerry maneuvered his way through the heavy Atlanta traffic and finally reached the ramp to I-20. The busy interstate highway represented the way out of populated Atlanta to destinations west. Just outside of the city he exited onto Highway 78 and headed for Birmingham, Alabama, just a couple of hours away. He planned to go north and west of that city to an area where there would be few people to question him. He had decided earlier that he was going to take the less traveled road though he liked the comfort, convenience and speed of the interstate highway system. He had had enough of the big city and the pressures of a high profile career. He also thought the scenic route might help him loosen up and forget the terrible strain he was under. It may be good therapy, he thought. Besides, traffic had increased on I-20 and it was constantly under repair.

Jerry relaxed somewhat as the pick up truck sped along the lonely road. The sun was quickly burning away the early morning fog and, except for a few clouds, it looked as if it would be a beautiful day. The road was in relatively good repair and offered a smooth ride, although Jerry wished the pavement was a bit wider. He looked out his window at the tall Georgia pines planted row after row. A sign indicated they had been planted some eighteen years earlier. On the right was green rolling pasture land with a lake at the bottom and cows dotting the hills, grazing. He passed a large man-made lake where two adolescent boys, presumably skipping school, were getting into a boat with their fishing poles.

After a few minutes on the lonely country road a light rain began to fall. Jerry looked up through the windshield and saw a dark cloud hovering over the area but decided it would pass and left the window down. The cool morning air flowed through the truck. Mid-April offered cool mornings and warm afternoons. He looked in the rear view mirror and saw Blue, his mouth blown into a smile, standing in the truck body. Jerry smiled and reached over to make sure his cellular phone was operational. As much as he was trying to get away from it all, he still wanted to stay in touch just in case the President needed to get through to him. He replaced the phone and looked up just in time to see a tall, lanky man who looked to be in his fifties on the side of the road with his thumb out. It was against Jerry's better judgment to pick up strangers, something he preached to Mary Ann and Alison that they should never do, but for some reason he felt compelled to stop.

He slowed the vehicle and pulled over to the ditch and stopped about a hundred yards beyond the man. Jerry looked in the mirror and watched as the man jogged toward the truck. Jerry slowly backed up a ways to let him know that he was going to pick him up.

Blue yapped at the big stranger when he threw his bag in the back of the truck. He patted the big dog on the head and said, "Good boy," pulled open the passenger side door and poked his head in.

"Where are you headed?" Jerry asked.

"Well, where are you headed?" the man countered in a pleasant tone.

Jerry was caught off guard with the inquiry. "Uh, I'm going west, on the other side of Birmingham, a couple of hours from here."

"That sounds fine to me," the man agreed. He slid onto the seat and put his hand out. He had a friendly smile and the most beautiful blue eyes Jerry had ever seen. "My name is Caleb."

"Mine is Jerry Watson." He put his hand forward and it was immediately swallowed up by the gigantic hand. There was a warmth that shot straight up Jerry's arm and into his heart. Wow! he thought. There is something different about this guy.

"Well sir, I sure appreciate your picking me up. It looks like it might rain again."

"Yes it does." Jerry peered over the steering wheel and into the darkened sky. He checked to see if the way was clear, then pulled back onto the road. "But I don't remember it raining any time recently."

"Is that right?" Caleb looked out his window quizzically. "I was quite a ways from here last night and it sure poured down there."

"Where was that?" Jerry asked.

"Oh, I was up around Grand Rapids. I had to pay a visit to someone up there."

"Grand Rapids? Michigan?" Jerry queried.

"That's a long way from Atlanta and this Georgia back road. How did you manage to get here in such a short period of time, and what are you doing out in the middle of nowhere?"

"Well, I guess you might say I'm lucky." The older man replied. "I caught a ride just after sunset with a trucker that was bound for Florida. I went to sleep and when I woke up we were stopped at a truck stop on I-75. He must have stopped to fill up and get something to eat because he wasn't in the cab, so I went to the restroom. When I returned to the spot where the truck was parked he was gone. I finally caught a ride with an old man who lives somewhere out here in these woods. I must have misunderstood him because I thought he was staying on the interstate, but he ended up out here. When he said he was going further west, I decided I'd get out and take my chances."

The stranger looked straight ahead and Jerry eyed him for a moment. He did not look like most hitchhikers he had seen who were unkempt and sometimes in ragged clothing. He was neat and clean. It did not seem possible he could have gotten this far in twelve hours. Something did not add up about his story and Jerry remembered his many warnings to his daughter and wife. It was too late now, but Jerry wished he had not picked up the man. Although he seemed harmless, and there was a gentleness and peace about him, Jerry's original plan was to be by himself so he could get away from people. He decided he would keep a close eye on him, and ask a few more questions.

"Where are you from?"

"Mr. Jerry," Caleb began and turned and looked at him with the beautiful eyes filled with both kindness and energy, " I don't have a place I call home, I'm from all over. I've seen a lot of the world in my long tenure on this earth." He paused and he seemed to have read Jerry's thoughts when he continued, "I'm much older than the fifty to sixty year old man that I appear, sir. I keep myself in shape by exercising and eating right."

"Then where are you going?" Jerry pushed for an answer.

"Where are you going?" was his only reply.

"I told you I'm going west," Jerry reminded him.

The older man looked at him and a soft smile curled his lips. "Well, that's where I'm going."

Jerry turned his attention to the road and wondered about this unusual person who just happened to be standing alongside the road that Jerry was riding along on this particular day in April. Goose bumps rose on his arms and Jerry hoped the man did not sense his anxiety.

Jerry reached down and checked his phone once again and noticed from the corner of his eye that the stranger was looking at the phone. "It's handy to have, just in case of emergency," he answered Caleb's unspoken question.

"Yeah, they didn't have those things back in the old days."

"Just what did you do for a living, back *in the old days*?" Jerry asked.

"I did a lot of things, some people called me a 'Jack of all trades'. But mostly I've been in the business of helping people. That's what I like to do."

"And how do you do that?" Jerry asked.

"Well, I ...."

Beeeeeep!

Jerry reached over and picked up the receiver of the car phone. "Jerry Watson."

"Jerry. This is Ted Wynatt with the Secretary of State's office. Jan Thaggard gave me your number. I hope you don't mind my calling, it's important, Secretary Banes asked me to call."

"No, I don't mind Ted. What can I do for you?" Secretary of State Wilson Banes was one of Jerry's favorite cabinet members. And Jerry and Ted Wynatt, Secretary Banes' top aide, had become good friends in the couple of years they had known each other.

"First of all Jerry, I want you to know I'm not one of your enemies, I've worked with you long enough to know you are a man of integrity. But there are some in this administration who are out to get you. I believe the President needs you, and the President believes that too, I just hope he can get past the personal attacks and not be forced to make drastic decisions to please the poll takers. You know this is an election year."

"Thanks, Ted. It is good to know there are still some people in Washington who believe in me. I want to continue to help the President if I can." Jerry glanced over at his passenger and noticed his inquisitive look.

"We have a sticky problem with Chile's attempt to become part of the Western Hemisphere Trade Agreement presently being worked out by our negotiating team in South America." Ted continued. "The basic problem is we don't want to go back to the Congress for approval on import quotas, the way things are right now the President doesn't think it would be a good idea. We believe we have the authority to exempt Chile's soy bean crop from the quotas, and it looks like that is the only way they are going to be able to sell it to their legislative body. But we want to be sure we're on good legal ground–no need to go through any unnecessary pain. Anyway, I know you're going out of town, but I don't need your review until the first of next week."

"I see." Jerry listened intently for several minutes as Ted Wynatt detailed the problem with the soy bean quotas.

"Ted, have your secretary fax a copy of the article to my office and I'll take a look at it first thing Saturday morning when I return. I'll call you and let you know what I think about it. Then you can run it by your people at State and see what they think." Jerry finished the conversation and placed the phone in its cradle. He did not have the stomach to think about the White House, Congress, or anything connected to the Beltway at the moment. He just wanted some space. He was not even sure if he would be back in the office on Saturday, or any day, for that matter.

"Mr. Jerry, I didn't mean to listen in on your conversation, but it sounds like you are an important person."

"Oh, I don't know about that." Jerry wasn't being modest, he just did not feel very important.

"It's none of my business, but I gather that you've got something to do with the President."

Jerry was not one to tell his personal business to anyone, especially a complete stranger, and not knowing who or what he was made it even riskier. He wondered about the man sitting next to him. What if this guy has a gun and decides to kidnap me for ransom? He remembered the .38 under the seat and wished he had it a little closer.

The older man leaned over and asked, "How did you become an advisor to the most powerful man in the world?"

"I don't remember telling you I was an advisor to the President." Jerry shot back.

The stranger jumped back in his seat and chuckled, "Well, you're right about that Mr. Jerry. But don't forget I did overhear your conversation, and though I'm an old man, I can still add 2 and 2. You don't have to tell me, I was just curious."

Jerry took his eyes off the road for a moment and observed the old man once more. He was dressed in an old but clean pair of Levis, a western denim shirt with embroidery near the top, and a pair of new Nike tennis shoes. His light brown hair which was thinning on top had a tinge of red in it and he had 1970s style sideburns. His face was thin with a protruding chin, a bit weathered but clean shaven. He had no striking features, except his eyes. They were a combination of energy and compassion. There was an aura about this man that both frightened and lifted Jerry. He knew he would tell him more if he asked again.

The stranger turned to Jerry once again and said, "It's up to you if you want to tell me."

As if on cue Jerry cleared his throat and began, "I worked in the campaign of a North Carolina congressman while I was in Law school at Duke University and from that experience I developed a keen interest in politics. I also had a desire to pursue a career in international law as a result of time I spent in the Orient as an exchange student. When I graduated I was hired by a firm in Washington, D. C. and worked my way up the ranks. Eventually I developed an international clientele and moved back to my favorite city in the whole world, Atlanta, Georgia. I was sought out by presidential candidate Kenneth Morton as an advisor. He won the election, mostly because of his economic platform. So that's how I got where I am today."

"That's a very interesting story, Mr. Jerry.

You must enjoy your work and life."

"Yeah," was Jerry's only reply.

Jerry brought the pick up truck to a stop at an intersection where two lonely country roads met. Jerry pulled a road map from the glove compartment and checked it to make sure he was on the road to Birmingham. Although he had traveled this way a couple of times, he was not that familiar with the particular road and the map did not indicate an intersection. The roads on the map became a blur as Jerry stared at it. He was unable to make a decision as to which way to go. Blue yapped from the back of the truck as if to say, "Let's get going again."

"Mr. Jerry?" Caleb tugged at his sleeve. "Is something wrong?"

"Huh?"

"Are you going to go on?"

"Uh, yes. This map seems to be outdated and I'm not sure which way to go."

"Why don't you go this way," he pointed to the narrow black top to the right. "I think it will take you where you need to go."

Jerry was puzzled. How did the stranger know which way to go? But something in Caleb's tone of voice convinced Jerry to go in the direction he pointed. He pulled onto the road and soon they were back up to the speed limit. By now the mid-morning sun was getting a little warm so Jerry rolled his window all the way down. Blue was standing up again and taking in the cool breeze.

After a few miles of silence Jerry stated, "The truck has been pulling to the right for the last several miles. I may need some air in the tire, but I don't believe there's going to be a station out here."

"Look! Isn't that a station?" Caleb was hunched forward near the dash and pointed his long finger once again.

"It looks like some kind of business. I think those are gas pumps out front."

He pulled off the narrow two lane highway and stopped in front of a lone country store located about 25 feet off the road. Two freshly painted but outdated gas pumps stood about ten feet apart on a gas island and directly across from the front doors of the store–a gable roof extended out over the pumps. Advertisements for meat, bread, and vegetables adorned the windows. An antiquated looking Coca Cola sign stood on top of the overhang.

The concrete block building was bright yellow and sported a new tin roof. The property was landscaped with lavender hydrangeas, elephant ears, beautiful azaleas, and a Y shaped trellis which allowed a climbing rose bush to run its full length of some seven feet. Near the front door of the residence was a big picture window with blue and white trimmed curtains. A TV antenna near the front door was anchored to the side of the roof with metal strapping. At the end of the house a screened porch ran the width of the building. Approximately one third of it looked to be the grocery store with the remaining portion apparently serving as a residence for the owners.

A small creek flowed along the south end of the property and then down a deep ravine until it disappeared in thick brush. Two boys about nine and eleven wearing cut off jeans, and with bare feet and no shirts, were rolling a tire in the side yard.

Jerry poked his head out of his window and hollered to the two boys, "Do you have any air here?"

"Yes sir," the bigger one replied. "Over there by that there shed." He pointed to a lean-to attached to the side of the store. He and his friend returned to their game and rolled the tire toward the creek. A rusty compressor was situated under the shelter and a rubber hose protruded from it. Jerry pulled his truck over the gravel drive to the air compressor.

"I'll air it up for you," Caleb said as the two men stepped onto a bed of small pebbles.

Jerry stood beside the truck and watched the two boys skip toward the creek.

"Got it all aired up," Caleb stated and stood to his full height.

"Let's go in and see if they have anything to eat here. Doesn't look like there are any restaurants way out here and I didn't have breakfast." Jerry said. He patted Blue on the head, "Stay here, boy. We'll bring you something in a few minutes."

When they walked past the gas pumps Jerry noticed they were the old type with the wind up arm on the side and the glass bubble in the middle that spun around like a top. They bore little resemblance to the computerized version he had left in Atlanta. He couldn't quite make out the price, but he thought it was $.22 a gallon. Must be $1.22, he decided.

He stepped onto the concrete pad under the porch and reached to open one of the double doors for Caleb. "Oh! Look at the screen protectors on the bottom of the doors–it's Little Miss Sunbeam." The brightly colored metal protectors were the kind his step-daddy had placed on the front doors of his store when Jerry was a boy. Sure enough, there was Little Miss Sunbeam, the mascot of the bread company with the pretty blonde hair, lovely smile, and blue dress. It was Jerry's favorite bread and he instantly remembered the commercials that proudly stated it was batter whipped. As a boy Jerry tried many times the test of tearing a slice in two, and it tore evenly every time, as advertised.

He stepped inside the store and immediately experienced the smell and sights of the past. He felt weak as he stood there and took it all in. "Is something wrong?" Caleb asked.

"Uh, I don't know yet," Jerry managed to say.

The surroundings held him captive, memories flooded him as he looked down at the dusty wood floor and the shelving which ran from top to bottom on the wall to his left. The shelves were well stocked with canned goods such as pork and beans, cream corn, green beans, peaches, carnation milk, Vienna sausages, and other items. Large bags of rice and flour were on the bottom shelf. Boxes of washing powders were on the floor. Higher up were the tobacco products–cigarettes, cigars, cans of snuff and plug chewing tobacco. It was odd, but all of the products were displayed in outdated packaging. Could business be this slow in these parts?

A metal bread rack was positioned just to his right and Jerry could smell the fresh cinnamon rolls, bread, and cakes. He immediately spotted the old fashioned multilayered coconut cakes his grandma used to buy. Directly in front of him was a counter with a cash register, a box of Bazooka bubble gum, assorted candy and cookies in jars, a large jar of pickled pig's feet, and other items. Next to the counter was a red chest type Coca Cola case. A clankety metal fan sitting on the counter put out a faint breeze in the warm room.

"Looks a little on the musty side I'd say." Caleb observed.

"It's amazing."

"What's that?" Caleb asked.

"It looks a lot like my step-daddy's country

30

store, except he had a bar on the side."

"Howdy!" a voice from behind the counter called out. A plump but pleasant woman stood from her stooping position and flashed a snaggle toothed smile. "Not too many people come this way. You folks from Atlanta?"

"Yes." Jerry continued to look around the room. "Yes we are."

To the woman's right was a meat case. Jerry stepped over the wooden floor and it creaked under his weight. He peered through the window of the case and admired the pork chops, ham, and sirloin steak on display."

"Hey, look! My favorite–bologna. And it's packaged in a roll. You don't see it packaged that way these days. Can you get me some of that baloney?" He asked the lady who was making her way around the case.

"Shore, how much you want?"

"Give me about a a half pound, thick sliced."

The old lady took the roll out of the case and carried it to a chopping block where she used a sharp knife to carve off several slices of bologna, leaving a small end piece. When she had cut approximately one half pound she threw it up on a set of scales on white waxed paper. "Looks like about a half a pound," she said and then wrapped it in brown meat wrapping paper. She turned to the counter and reached for a spool of twine, unrolled some and tied up the package.

"Here you go." she said and handed it to him.

"Uh, do you mind if I have that too?" He pointed to the end piece which was laying on the meat block. "My brother and I used to fight over the end piece when we were kids. I haven't seen one of those in years."

"Sure mister, you can have it. I was just gonna throw it away."

"I'd also like a loaf of your white bread, 2 cokes, and I want that coconut cake over there." he said pointing to the metal rack with the bread items on it.

The old lady made her way to the bread rack and got a loaf of bread and the cake. She plodded back behind the drink box, opened it from the top and pulled out two cokes. "Do you want these opened?" she asked.

"Yes." Jerry reached in his pocket and pulled out a $20 bill. "How much?"

The old woman looked at the money and laughed, "I ain't seen one of them in a while."

"Let me take care of that." Caleb stepped in between Jerry and the woman and handed her some change. "It's the least I can do."

"But that doesn't look like it is enough."

"Let's see." She scratched some figures on a piece of paper and rung up the purchase on her NCR cash register. "That's just about right." She took the money and gave Caleb a few coins, then opened the drinks with a bottle opener.

"Do you mind if we sit on that seat over there and eat?" Jerry pointed to a cushioned settee against the wall.

"Naw, go right ahead. Put this coin in that there juke box and play your favorite song."

"Juke box?" he asked.

"Yeah. That one over there in the corner next to the bar stools."

Sure enough, a juke box was located in the rear of the room, and a wood counter which apparently served as a bar, about forty two inches high and eight feet long. Several wooden stools were positioned in front of the bar. Jerry took the coin and turned to Caleb and they both proceeded to the seat near the juke box. They sat down and put the bologna between two slices of bread and hungrily tore into their sandwiches and washed them down with some of the best tasting coke he had ever drunk.

After Jerry had finished the sandwich and taken a few bites from the cake he turned to Caleb and said, "I'm going to try that juke box." Jerry read the instructions and said, "Caleb, come here and look."

"What is it?" Caleb jumped up and stood by his side.

"Look at these songs–there's He'll Have To Go by Jim Reeves, and The Battle of New Orleans by Johnny Horton, and El Paso by Marty Robbins."

He selected *He'll Have To Go.* The cylinder rotated to the appropriate place, the mechanical arm raised up and made its selection, and evenly laid the 45 RPM record on the spinning turntable, the needle came down cleanly on the record and out came the rich, deep voice of Jim Reeves. The juke box glowed with its multicolored lights flashing on and off. Jerry was transfixed by the rich sound of the music and the blinking lights. He stared into the yellow, orange, and red lights until he merged with the music and the colors.

3

The flashing colors mesmerized Jerry, and for a moment he thought he heard his mother call out his name. "Jerry!" his mother called. "Get out of here right now. I done told you to stay out of this place."

The red, yellow, and orange lights of the juke box blinked on and off like it did every Saturday afternoon at Last Stop. It had captivated Jerry f35or hours on the lazy summer afternoon while he sat on the wooden floor in front of the big plastic and metal box. The country songs of the day by Kitty Wells, Jim Reeves, Ernest Tubb, and George Jones bellowed out loud across the room. The few patrons of the establishment kept the music flowing as they put in their coins, selected the number and letter of the song they wanted to hear, and then went back to the bar stool from where they came. Jerry watched the canister of 45 RPM records rotate around to the proper location, then the mechanical arm methodically selected the right record, brought it forward, and laid it softly on the turntable. The turntable rotated and the needle fell lightly on the exact spot to begin the song. This time it was "White Lightning" by George Jones.

"Now you go on." Lettie Watson came over to where he was sitting and stooped over, pulled him by the arm and gave the six year old a swat on the behind. He jumped up and sprinted to the adjoining room which served as living quarters for Charlie Watson, his wife Lettie, and four stepsons–Dale, Jerry, Jeremy and Justin.

Last Stop Beer and Groceries was a simple block building located about three miles outside of Washburn on a country blacktop. The grocery store was located in the front of the building and the bar occupied the back. The Juke Joint comprised a small area consisting of a counter, bar stools and juke box on wooden floor, and plain beige walls. Beer signs with bright neon lights hung in the windows. Table displays, with beer glasses bubbling up colored water to simulate a cool drink, sat on the counter.

Once Jerry's mother was off to another part of the store, he sneaked back in the bar and hid behind the old car seat which was used as a couch. He peeked once again at the men who were patronizing the bar on this Saturday afternoon.

"Aaaa-haaa," the high pitched, guttural sound of Virgil wafted through the room.

"Aaaa-haaaa," The sound rang out once again. Virgil was short, balding, and quiet. He always wore brown slacks that were a bit too long, brown lace up shoes, and a white shirt with no tie. Jerry watched him intently. He sat for hours at Last Stop and drank his favorite beer, Miller High Life. Jerry watched as he puckered his lips and brought the bottle up close like he was preparing to kiss his best girl. He did not move much, nor did he talk, he just sat there looking into space as if he was trying to forget a lost love or a business venture that went sour. Finally he slowly rose from the wooden stool, wobbled over to the juke box, put in the appropriate coins and selected his favorite song. He made his way back to the stool just in time to raise the bottle, purse his lips and, just as the music started, "Aaaa-haaa!"

Virgil put the bottle down on the counter, a loud belch escaped his lips and he made a face as his

36

sour breath reached his nostrils. He turned his head to the side and spotted little Jerry out of the corner of his eye. He knew he would be hiding behind the seat, he was always there. Virgil pretended he did not see him, then suddenly he sprung forward with his arms outstretched and shouted, "Waaaaaaaa!"

Jerry shrieked and covered his face with his hands.

"Ha ha haaaaa," Virgil laughed and staggered forward. He nearly lost his balance, and grabbed the counter for support. He regained his feet and settled back on the stool. "Thought you could sneak up on me, didn't you son?" He slurred his words and cocked his head slightly as he looked down at the boy.

Jerry sat paralyzed with most of his body behind the seat and did not say a word. Scrunched up in a ball, arms around his knees, he looked up at the red faced man. Virgil reached for the dark beer bottle, a wedding band was on his stubby finger but he did not have a wife, at least that is what his mother had told Jerry.

"Get an education son." He began on his favorite theme. "Get an education. Can't nobody take it away from you. Can't nobody take advantage of you neither." He belched another loud belch and thumped his bottle down spilling a few drops on the wooden counter top.

"I been working at that lumber mill 22 years. Kept the books for 'em. Ain't nobody better. And you know what they did? They hired a kid with a college degree. Paid him more than me. It just ain't right." He shook his head from side to side. Virgil turned to Jerry and lowered his head to eye level. "Are you listening, boy?" he growled.

Jerry could smell his breath and nearly choked on the pungent scent. "I said, can you hear me, boy?" He swatted at him and nearly caught Jerry in the face but he moved his head to the side quickly. He felt the brush of his hand.

"Y-y-y-yes sir," he responded.

"Then what did I say?"

Jerry tightened in a ball and swallowed hard. He opened his mouth but no air would pass through his lips. He had a sick feeling in the pit of his stomach. He tried to speak again but nothing came out.

"I said, What did I say." His face was closer and redder, his breath was sour and made Jerry sick.

"Get an education, Jerry blurted out, unrolled his body and darted past the blundering drunk as he clumsily tried to grab him.

"Aaahhhaahahahahahaha," Virgil laughed and laughed.

Jerry ran as fast as he could, pumping his legs as fast as they would carry him through the store and toward the double doors. Suddenly he smacked into someone and fell backwards. "Aaahhhh," he yelled and tumbled to the hard wood floor.

"What ya doin' boy?" The man in khaki pants and cowboy hat muttered. Jerry had run into Charlie Watson, the tall red-headed man to whom his mother was married. Jerry was only three years old when his real father died of a heart attack and Charlie became the only father he knew. Charlie resented the attention Lettie gave her boys and he vented his frustration against them, especially Jerry. Fear gripped him as he lay sprawled on the floor.

"Come here." The man reached down and grabbed Jerry by his shirt and said, "You're goin' with me. I done told you to stay away from my people. Now let me show you what you're gonna end up being."

He jerked Jerry to his feet and dragged him

through the grocery store. Several Saturday afternoon grocery customers stopped to see what the commotion was about. Everybody in the small town of Washburn knew Charlie Watson was a drinker, and it was rumored that he mistreated his family, but people kept shopping at his grocery store because he offered something most of them could not get elsewhere–credit. Jerry remained silent as Charlie yanked on his shirt and kicked the screen doors open on his way to his pick up truck. Charlie opened the door and threw him in the cab.

Jerry could hardly think as he bounced along in the rusty Chevy which made its way along the gravel road that ran next to Last Stop. Jerry knew immediately where they were going. Neither of them said anything on the short trip to Lester Cone's, the biggest bootlegger in town. It was no secret and he had been busted many times by Beverage Agents. But he kept getting out of jail and selling his illegal whiskey to men like Charlie.

"Yeah boy," Charlie sucked on a Salem and drew the menthol smoke deep into his lungs. "Ain't nothing like a little whiskey to make you forget things." He gripped the steering wheel with both hands and rocked back and forth in his seat enjoying the ride. He cut his eye toward Jerry and exhaled in his direction. The smoke nauseated him and made his eyes water, but he swallowed hard and held back the temptation to cough.

"Haw haw!" He inhaled again and blew it directly at Jerry, then jerked his hat off and fanned toward him. "You can't take it can you boy?"

Suddenly Jerry wheezed and coughed and bent double trying to relieve the itchy feeling in his throat.

"Haw haw! You ain't never gonna amount to nothin'. You're gonna be just like the rest of us rednecks. You're gonna smoke, drink whiskey, and do nothin' with your life. Maybe you'll be like this bootlegger we're fixin' to see, he ain't got no education. He's gotta sell illegal whiskey for a living." The older Watson laughed and whipped the truck to the right and onto a graded road which was not big enough for two vehicles. Charlie slowly rode past a frame house where several children were playing on a junk car in the side yard. Two more kids were swinging on a rope tied to an oak tree. As the mufflerless truck made its presence known another child dashed from inside the house to the front porch and peered at them from a large hole in the screen door.

Charlie surveyed the area as he passed the house. The truck sputtered down the road about a quarter of a mile to an opening with thick brush on either side and a gate which led into an open field. The older man swung into the narrow drive, stopped, slammed the truck in reverse, and headed back toward Leroy's. The children were still staring as they made another pass of the house. Then Charlie turned and drove alongside the house on a two rut trail with brush and trees on one side and a dilapidated fence on the side nearest the house. About fifty yards into the well beaten path he stopped the truck and switched off the motor. In a few minutes a young woman appeared on the back porch, stepped down the rickety steps, and made her way toward the truck with two mangy dogs following. When she got close enough to recognize the driver she stopped and stared at him until he raised his forefinger. The girl turned and went back to the house. Jerry understood the procedure the two just went through, they had done it many times before. In a few minutes the young woman returned to the trail and this time she strode all the way to Charlie's window. She did not say anything but simply pulled a bottle of whiskey from under her blouse and handed it to him. He took the bottle and put it beside Jerry on the seat. It was Seagram's Seven, Charlie's favorite, mainly because it was the only thing Leroy sold, and it was cheap.

"Thank ya, pretty lady." He slipped her a bill which she folded and placed in her blouse. She turned and headed toward the house, her bare feet staying on the clearing and avoiding the weeds and high grass on either side of the trail. The same dogs who greeted her earlier followed faithfully along. Charlie backed the truck out of the trail and onto the graded road. Just before he reached the broader and smoother gravel road he stopped the truck once again, grabbed the bottle, and twisted off the cap. Jerry watched as he tilted his head, placed the bottle to his lips and took a long swig of the alcohol. "Aarrhhgg," Charlie exhaled with a cough, his eyes watered, his face contorted. Then he raised the bottle for another drink.

"How come you drink that stuff if it tastes so bad?" Jerry was shocked at his boldness.

Charlie yanked the bottle from his lips and threw a startled look at Jerry. "Who are you to question me? You ain't nothing, never have been, and never will be." He snapped his hand out toward the boy and caught him on the left ear. Jerry ducked and threw up his hands but was unable to avoid the stinging blow of the elder Watson's long fingers. He winced in pain and withdrew to the far side of the truck cab.

They were still sitting on the narrow road and Charlie pushed the whiskey bottle to the boy, "Here! Take a drank," he ordered.

"I don't want none."

"I said drank it." He strained toward the boy

41

clutching the bottle in his right hand and holding onto the steering wheel with his left. He glared at him and hollered, "I said drank it."

"I don't want none." The little boy yelled from behind the shield of his hands. The long arm of Charlie Watson snapped out once again and hit Jerry on top on his head.

"Owwww!" Jerry yelled. Again the big hand lashed out and caught the boy on the mouth. "Please don't hit me no more," Jerry sobbed and held his head in his hands.

"I said drank this whiskey or I'll beat the daylights out of ya." Charlie switched hands and held the bottle in his left hand while he reached farther with his right and grabbed Jerry by the back of his neck. He guided his head to the bottle, and put it to his mouth as Jerry struggled to break free. "Drank it." Charlie forced the boy's mouth on the opening and turned the bottle up. The strong drink gushed out and spilled down Jerry's T-shirt and some into his mouth. It burnt harshly on its way down his throat. He finally broke free of Charlie's grip and gasped and wheezed for breath as he doubled over.

"Haw, haw, haw." Charlie jumped back behind the wheel, threw it in first gear and roared down the gravel road. "You ain't nothin' and never will be." He sneered at him. "You better get used to drankin' whiskey cause that's what you're gonna do the rest of your life."

After the incident at Leroy's Jerry hid in his room and avoided Charlie for the rest of the day. The next morning he awoke to the usual cursing and hollering that he experienced every day–it was Charlie screaming at Lettie because she did not cook his eggs the way he liked them.

After breakfast Charlie went to town and

Jerry came out of his room and sat down at the kitchen table. "Why do you stay with him?" he heard himself ask.

The question startled Lettie but she answered. "Son, there are four of you boys and I need help raisin' you. Charlie may not be the best man in the county but at least he's willing to give us a place to live and something to eat."

The words stunned Jerry. He sat at the table and stared into space for a long time. ...

"Mr. Jerry? Are you there?" Caleb pulled on his sleeve.

"Huh?" Jerry shook his head and looked around at the musty surroundings. The juke box had finished the last song and the arm was going back into place.

"Where have you been the last few minutes?"

"I don't know. I need to get some air Caleb, I'll be back in a few minutes."

Jerry spotted a door at the back of the building and headed toward it. He opened the screen door and stepped onto the concrete block steps and into the back yard. He surveyed an area of about twenty five feet by forty feet, the grass was freshly mown. There were several trees spotting the yard, two lawn chairs and a small round table on a patio. A trellis with rose bushes running up its length provided some shade from the sun. Jerry sat down in one of the chairs and took a deep breath. His mind was working over time. The place had a mesmerizing effect on him which he could not explain. It was uncanny. It was as if he had been taken back into time.

While he pondered matters he looked up and saw the two boys he had seen earlier. They

43

were running for the corner of the yard, laughing and playing. The big boy ran ahead of the smaller one who yelled, "I'm gonna get you for that."

"Aw, come on Timmy, it was just a frog." The bigger boy laughed and turned toward him. "Come on let's go play in the tent."

"What!" Jerry gasped when he looked into the corner of the yard and spied a tent made of quilts.

4

"Man, I hate Salems." Jerry sucked in the menthol smoke and exhaled it quickly and rolled over next to his best friend George Turner.

"Hey! Watch it. This thing you call a tent ain't nothing but your mama's quilts hanging over a limb and chairs. You don't want it falling on us." George scooted over a few inches. "You might hate the taste of menthols but right now its the best we got. And they sure are better than them butts we found in the ash trays yesterday. I am tired of straightening them things out and smoking them."

"Yep! But as long as old Charlie lays drunk on the bed we will be well supplied."

"Yeah." George laughed. "Your old man sure is stupid. I can't believe he ain't figured out that we get a pack and pull one forward in the carton to look like its full.

"Hey, Jerry. Are you excited about the first day of school next week?" George asked, puffing lightly on the cigarette.

"Naa! I don't have time for school. I think I'll go fishing down at Mr. Townsend's pond." Jerry rolled over on his belly, drew again on the cigarette, and breathed out the bluish smoke into a flock of gnats. "Ahhh! Dog Days in South Georgia–heat, high humidity, gnats and flies."

"You done missed about a thousand days of school, and failed one year because of it. How you ever gonna pass? "

"It don't matter no how. My old man told

me that I'm never gonna amount to nothing. I think I'll just be what he says—no good."

"Well, I can't wait. We finally get to sixth grade, King of the Hill at Washburn Elementary. Man, just think about it, we get to do what we want on the playground." George rolled over and a big smile grew over his face.

"You ain't gonna be King of the Hill, you idiot." Jerry thumped him on the head. "You can't even smoke a cigarette without vomiting." Jerry laughed. "I heard your mama say to my mama the other day, 'I just can't understand why Georgie gets so sick every time he goes over to play with Jerry.'"

"Well, at least I'll be bigger than the guys in the other grades." He countered. "Besides, Mrs. Richardson is going to be our teacher. My brother Ben said she's the best in the world. She gives prizes to students who don't miss a day all year. She takes everybody on field trips, and she tells everybody she loves them, and how special they are."

"George you done gone soft on me. Teachers telling you that they love you." Jerry snickered. "How corny can you get?" Jerry blew out the smoke that he had breathed into his lungs seconds earlier. As he gazed up at a spider making her home in the ladder which served as the center pole of the tent—a belly ache made its way up into his throat. He had made fun of George but deep down inside he wanted what Mrs. Richardson gave her students. Jerry knew about her classes because three years before Dale had her as his teacher. It was a miracle. Dale was never a top student before sixth grade, or after, but somehow he made excellent grades that one year. He loved Mrs. Richardson and it was obvious she had made an impression on him. His mom was surprised but thankful and gave him a party at year's end for his performance. Charlie did not come to the party, he thought it was stupid and loudly declared it to the family. ...

Jerry had a secret desire to be someone important one day. He would dress up in a shirt and tie and pretend to be a lawyer trying a well known case. He knew lawyers were respected and that is what he wanted. He never shared his dream with anyone until one day when he was ten and he happened to find Charlie in a good mood. The two of them were in the back yard picking up beer bottles and cans which had accumulated over several weekends. They loaded Charlie's old pickup and hauled them off to some abandoned property near their house and dumped them with the trash that others had put there.

On their way home things were going very well. The two of them were talking about a subject they both enjoyed–the Green Bay Packers. "I believe Bart Starr is going to have his best game of the year against the Bears this Sunday. How'd you like to be a football player one day?"

"I don't know. I kinda would like to be a lawyer."

Suddenly Charlie guffawed and began to hit the steering wheel and peered over at Jerry. "You won't even go to school boy, how do you expect to be something as important as a lawyer? That's funny boy." He continued laughing all the way home. Jerry was embarrassed and humiliated by that event and vowed he would never again share his innermost desires with anyone.

Now he did not want to think about school anymore and sat up. He pulled the end of his cigarette off and poked it in the dirt underneath the quilt he was sitting on, and placed the butt in an old

Marlboro box top he had fished out of the trash can. He jumped up and said. "Let's get outta here. Talking about school makes my stomach queasy." ...

"Students, I want to welcome you to sixth grade. This will be your last experience in elementary school and I want to help you make it your best year yet." Mrs. Richardson stood in front of the blackboard in a blue skirt and white blouse, navy high heels, and gold earrings dangling from her ears. She had shoulder length brown hair, and stood tall. Jerry's mama told him she was about fifty years old but she did not look that old to him.

The classroom was just big enough for the twenty five desks, the teacher's desk, and a couple of tables in the back at which students could work or play. On one side was a row of windows where Jerry's desk was fourth from the front. During the early fall and spring the windows were left open. On this August morning a blue jay had lighted on the window sill right by Jerry's desk and he was intently watching the bird's maneuverings while trying to listen to the teacher. He could not believe he was sitting there on the first day of school.

"Now students this year I am going to share many things that will help you be a success in life. If you will listen to me and study hard you will not only pass this grade, but you will pass every class you take in the future, and you will do well when you graduate from school." Mrs. Richardson made her way over toward Jerry's desk as she talked, she also saw the bird. "As a matter of fact Jerry Watson, my purpose as a teacher is to help you be a success in life. Did you know that?"

"Uh, no ma'am." Jerry was embarrassed. He was shy because he was ashamed of his past and of Charlie. He had failed a grade due to excessive absences and was at least a year older than the other kids, this made him uncomfortable. He squirmed a bit and rubbed his sweaty hands on his new dungarees. The other children chuckled as Jerry's face turned red.

"Don't be embarrassed Master Watson," she reassured him. "One day your school days will be over and you will enter the real world. You will be thankful that Mrs. Richardson drilled a few of these things into your head." Mrs. Richardson moved behind her desk, picked up a piece of chalk and stepped over to the blackboard. "Because school is for the purpose of training you for life, and not so your parents can get rid of you, or to give you something to do between summer vacations, I want to give you some good advice. Listen well and you will be prepared to live a productive and happy life."

"There are a few other things I want to tell you before I assign your books to you," Mrs. Richardson lowered her voice and leaned over her desk. There was a hush in the room. "I want everyone of you to know that I love you and I love teaching. I believe in everyone of you. There's not a student in this room that has to fail. You can do something special with your life."

Jerry had never heard anyone say this to him. He was used to Charlie cursing him and telling him how stupid he was. "You ain't never gonna amount to nothin'," was his favorite saying. Suddenly Mrs. Richardson looked different, she was prettier, and seemed taller. Jerry had wondered why Dale had done so well in sixth grade and now he was beginning to see why.

"One other thing," she continued. "I'll reward every student who is faithful in attendance in sixth grade. If you miss no more than two days the entire year you'll get a special prize." She reached inside her desk drawer and smiled broadly at the students.

She had everyone's attention by now, including Jerry's. He leaned forward, as did the other kids, to see what she was going to pull from the desk. She removed a paper bag and laid it on her desk. "The girls will get a brand new jump rope and set of jacks," she said as she pulled a new jump rope and set of jacks from the bag and held them up. The girls giggled and squealed their approval. Then she reached in the bag once more. "The boys will get a Barlow knife." She held the brown handled knife high for everyone to see. Several of the guys said, "All right!" with enthusiasm. The kids excitedly chattered away at how they would win the prize. The noise level increased but Jerry did not hear any of it, all he could think about was the knife. He stared intently while she waved it in front of the class. He made up his mind right then that he was going to get one of those Barlow knives. It never occurred to him that he had not been faithful to attend class in the past.

The first day went by quickly. There was little work to do but a lot of catching up with old friends and making new ones. Before he knew it the bell rang to go home and Jerry gathered up his books and belongings. As he did Mrs. Richardson came over to him and asked, "Jerry, may I talk with you?"

"Uh, yes ma'am." Jerry gulped. He looked up into her face and noticed the biggest and most beautiful smile he had ever seen.

"Jerry," she started. "I know about your past."

"Uh, you do?"

"Yes, I do." She took his hands in hers and looked right into his eyes. "I know you've missed a lot of school, and as a result you failed one year. I'm sure you feel funny about being the oldest kid in my class."

Jerry did not know what to say. She was right, he was embarrassed and hoped nobody said anything about his age, or his past, or his step-daddy. But how did she know how he felt? Down inside he wanted to be a good student and attend school. And he longed for the other students to like him.

"Jerry?" There was that beautiful voice once again. "I'm going to help you achieve this year. I believe in you and I know you can do it. There are very few like you and if you will listen to those special people God puts in your path, you will be a success beyond your wildest imaginations. You'll do great things and help many people. Jerry, if you are faithful to attend school this year, not only will you receive the Barlow knife, but you will receive something far more valuable." She released his hands and stepped back to look at him. Jerry's heart pounded and he felt like he did during Christmas holidays when his mother would put gifts under the tree but would not let the boys open them.

"But don't forget," Mrs. Richardson brought his attention back to their earlier discussion. "The grand prize will be revealed at the end of the year." She let his hands go and turned to her desk. "I'll see you tomorrow, Jerry."

Jerry waved goodbye from the door and skipped down the hall to the outside and on the path through the playground. I wonder what the grand prize is? he thought. He was halfway home before he dismissed it from his mind. But he could not forget the conversation, and he decided he was going to stick around school for a while, at least to see what happened next.

5

"Listen to me, students." Mrs. Richardson was standing in front of her class holding an American folk song book. She was smartly dressed in a black skirt, white blouse, and red scarf. Jerry gazed at her and for the first time wondered what it would be like to be married to her. She was kind and nice to him, like his mother, he wanted to be near her all the time. "It's time to get out your song books. We're going to start with 'Oh Susanna' on page 28."

Mrs. Richardson's class started each day with singing. It was fun and put everybody in a good mood. Jerry flipped the pages of his song book between his fingers until he found page 28. Suddenly he remembered it was Friday and he got a sick feeling in the pit of his stomach. On the last day of the week Mrs. Richardson called on individual students to sing solo. He hoped she did not call on him. He did not mind singing with everyone else because the other voices drowned him out, but he was embarrassed for the class to hear him sing. He slumped in his seat and tried to hide as much of his frame as he could. If he sat very still maybe she would not call on him.

"Today is the first day of solo singing." Mrs. Richardson moved slightly to her left and away from Jerry. He sighed a bit and watched her movements. "The reason we do this is so you'll gain confidence in standing before an audience. One day you'll be glad you had this experience and you'll send me a letter and thank me that I helped you overcome fear." She laughed and turned back toward Jerry. He sunk lower in his desk chair.

"We're going to start on the last row and our first singer will be Master Jerry Watson."

Terror gripped him–fear started in his legs and they began shaking. It crawled up his legs and into his belly, spread to his racing heart and into his throat where a big lump refused to move. He fidgeted uncomfortably in his seat.

"Oh Susanna don't you cry for me, I'm going to Alabama with a banjo on my knee..." The classroom singing could not drown out the whistles and rockets going off in Jerry's mind. He had dreaded this day since the first time she told the class they would have to sing. The group singing ended much too soon and Mrs. Richardson came right up to Jerry's desk and said, "Master Watson! Which song have you chosen?"

"Huh?"

"The song. Which song are you going to sing?"

"Oh!" Jerry snapped up. The students giggled and he felt his face burn with embarrassment. "I...I don't know," he gulped.

The other students were delighted with Jerry's uneasiness. The teacher recognized his dilemma and offered help. "How about 'Old Folks at Home', another Stephen Foster song on page 42?"

"Uh! Yes ma'am."

"Well come on and take center stage," she stepped back and made a sweeping gesture with her left hand indicating he had the floor.

Jerry slowly slipped out of his desk and stood before all the students and his teacher. He lifted his hanging head and gazed at the faces peering at him.

He swallowed hard and fought back the urge to run home, jump in his mama's arms and forget this awful experience. But his legs would not listen to his mind. His Keds tennis shoes remained frozen in place. Jerry opened his mouth and nothing came out. He tried again and a little croak slipped through his lips. The class roared in laughter and his face flushed and his knees weakened. Mrs. Richardson called down the children and regained order in the classroom. "Go ahead Jerry," she encouraged. "You can do it."

He attempted once again to sing and this time a cackle resonated from his chest, through his throat and out his mouth. "Way down upon the Suwannee River, far, far away...." There were giggles and some of the boys were making faces and gestures at him. Mrs. Richardson moved about the boys with her ruler and smacked a couple on the knuckles.

Jerry managed to get through the ordeal and found his seat. He was wet with perspiration; his heart was racing; he was spent; but he was happy. He had actually accomplished something.

"You did fine Jerry." Mrs. Richardson winked at him.

The singing every Friday was difficult for Jerry, but he continued to attend school faithfully. And then, when it was all over, Jerry was seated on the front row in the school auditorium with his classmates and all the other Washburn Elementary students. It was awards day, Jerry's first, and a day he had longed for since the first day of school. He anxiously waited through the awards and recognition given the younger students.

Finally Mr. Page, the principal, stood and introduced Mrs. Richardson. She gracefully ascended the stairs and stood behind the podium.

"It is my privilege to honor the 6th grade students who had perfect attendance this year. The girls are: Loretta Bryan, Sonya Thompson, and Jamie Williams. Please step forward and receive your rewards girls." The three girls made their way to the stage and gleefully grabbed their perfect attendance certificate and the jump rope and jacks Mrs. Richardson had promised in the beginning of the year. They ran back to their seats and proudly showed off their bounty to the other girls.

"Now I want the following boys to step forward and receive recognition for not missing one day this year. John Green, Tommy Sapp, George Turner, and Jerry Watson."

A rush went through Jerry's entire body. He actually thought he might not make it up the stairs. He had never experienced anything as thrilling as winning an award. He felt like his heart was going to burst through his chest. He looked out at the audience and saw George Turner's mom and dad, and the parents of the other boys, but neither his mother nor step-father was there. Charlie would not let his mama come because he did not think it was important. Jerry was disappointed but he made up his mind he was not going to let it dampen his spirits. He had achieved something, just like the day he finished the song, and he was proud. He gladly took the certificate and the prized Barlow knife from Mrs. Richardson's hand. She was smiling and bent over and gave him a hug. "I want to see you right after the ceremonies Jerry. I have something else to give you," she whispered.

"Yes ma'am." Jerry agreed, but he had what he wanted–the knife. He strode proudly back to his seat and he noticed some of the younger boys gazing admiringly at him. It was a strange feeling he had, one of accomplishment and pride, which he had never felt before. It was a good feeling to be admired by the younger kids. He sat down and listened as Mr. Page gave out several awards to teachers and staff. Soon it was over and everyone went back to his class.

There were lots of hugs and tears as the students said their goodbyes to each other. More than one person promised to write every week for the entire summer. Others excitedly discussed vacation plans, camp and summer schedules. But Mrs. Richardson got the most attention. While kids were hanging around her desk three girls were clinging to each other and sobbing at the thought of leaving her. "There'll never be another teacher like you," Loretta Bryan said as she tearfully gave her a big bear hug.

"I love you honey." Mrs. Richardson tenderly wiped away the tears from her cheeks and pulled the girl to herself again for another hug. The boys lined up to hug her and Jerry noticed some of them had tears in their eyes. He stood off to the side. He was determined he would not cry, but he did plan to hug her and tell her how much she meant to him.

As the other kids slowly had their say the line got shorter until there was only Jerry and Mrs. Richardson left. She reached out and held him at arm's length, eying him for the longest time. "Well, Master Jerry Watson. You did it, didn't you?"

"Yes ma'am. I did." He beamed.

She drew him close to her and gave him the tightest embrace he had ever received. He could smell her perfume and hear her heart beating. "I love you Jerry Watson and I'm proud of you. You're a special boy and I believe God has something great for you to do. And you have got what it takes to make it. You can do what you want to do, son."

He could not help it, but he burst into tears. Sobbing and crying like he had never experienced just flooded out of his soul. No one had ever talked to him that way. Besides his mother no one had ever loved him like Mrs. Richardson. But she added something his mother could not–encouragement and confidence to become a success. His mother did not have the emotional support or self esteem to instill in her children confidence to succeed. He sobbed loudly for several minutes and then stopped abruptly, pulled away and dried his face on his shirt. "I'm sorry," he muttered in embarrassment.

"That's okay son." She stroked his head. "What do you want to do when you grow up Jerry?"

He was hesitant to share with her, especially after what had happened with Charlie the day they were emptying trash. But after a few moments he went ahead. "I want to be a lawyer."

"Why do you want to become a lawyer?" she asked gently.

"Because I want to help people, and I want to be somebody important."

"Jerry," she took his left hand in her right hand. "I believe in you. I know you can succeed in what you want to become. I recognized it on you the first day of class. I want you to come with me." She walked out of the classroom and down the hall to a little used door. She reached for a key in her pocket and unlocked it. "Follow me," she said and started down a creaky stairway to a dimly lit and damp basement under her classroom. There was old furniture, books, used equipment and other items stored there. She led him to a corner where an old trunk was sitting against the wall. It had written on it "Mrs. Richardson 6th grade-Do not remove."

Mrs. Richardson sat in an antique secretary's chair beside the trunk and said, "Sit there," motioning to a folding chair. She took another smaller key, unlocked the trunk, opened it and gingerly reached into it. Jerry strained his neck as he leaned forward and peered at what must surely be a valuable article in the musty trunk. He soon discovered it was an ancient looking brown book, about the size of her hand, with *The Creed*. written across it.

"Jerry I keep this book in my trunk down here because I like to think of it as buried treasure. Coming down here seems to add a mysteriousness or adventure to it. It is in fact a kind of treasure, because in it are principles upon which a person can build his life and accomplish his wildest dreams. I don't bring everyone down here, but only those who I think will understand these principles and use them to benefit others. If you will keep these principles in your heart and guard them, one day you will succeed, not only for yourself, but so you can help others."

Jerry wondered what could be so powerful in the small, ordinary looking book. She placed it in her lap and opened it to the beginning. He leaned back in his chair and stared at a lone light bulb which offered her little help in reading the small book, but Mrs. Richardson did not need the light. She knew each word.

"Jerry, this book was written by one of the first Pilgrims who landed in New England three hundred years ago. The author is anonymous, maybe it was written by many, we don't know. But it was obvious to this great man, or men, that it would be very difficult for this nation to survive as free and prosperous unless certain principles were followed by its citizens. The author, or authors, believed it was imperative to build a country on character and principle and that individuals and families would be the backbone of this nation. He or they wrote these principles down, not for that generation, but for ours."

Jerry was not sure what this had to do with him, but he somehow understood what she was saying would one day help him, so he listened intently.

"Jerry, I know you're not interested in hearing me read this entire book to you, but I want to give you the essence of what it says. I'm going to condense it for you, and my prayer is that one day, when the time comes, you'll remember this meeting and you will be guided by these words." She shifted her weight in the squeaky chair and thumbed through the book. "There are four virtues the author proposes in *The Creed*, which he believed are essential to the continuation of a free society. They are: Have Faith in God; Get an Education; Work Hard; and Take Personal Responsibility for Your Actions."

"Hey! You talked about those kinds of things throughout the school year." Jerry piped up.

"That's right Jerry, you remembered." She smiled approvingly. "But many of the students have already forgotten. Some will come to understand this creed in later life, sadly, some will never grasp these principles. You may even forget them in your teenage years or early twenties, but the sooner you employ them in your life, the sooner you will get on the path to success."

Jerry could not quite comprehend everything, but he reasoned if she, an educated woman, believed in him, then maybe he did have something to offer, no matter what Charlie said.

"I want to briefly summarize the author's writings," she said and looked at her watch. "I know you want to go, this being the last day of school, so let's get started. The first principle is *Have Faith in God*. The early settlers and Founding Fathers of our country placed great faith in God. A strong belief in God will give you an advantage over those who don't believe in anything but themselves. You must realize there is a Higher Power that can give you strength and help in time of need. Jerry, I can't tell you how many times I've prayed and asked for Divine help to solve a problem. I've even asked for guidance in how I could help you."

Jerry was surprised by her confession. He did not know that much about religion, but he did feel something miraculous had happened in the past year. He had never before had perfect attendance.

"The second point is *Get an Education*." The pretty teacher moved toward Jerry and lowered her voice. "Now Jerry, it's very important that you listen to me. Your best chance to succeed in life is to get a good education. I've tried to instill in my students the importance of life long learning. No matter what you decide to do, be sure that you learn everything you can about it. The third quality is *Work Hard*," she continued. "This great country was forged by people who believed strongly that man can only advance by hard work; that there is no free lunch; and that anything worth having is worth working for. And fourth," she raised up again, "*Take Personal Responsibility for your Actions*. Do you understand what that means, Jerry?"

"I think it means something like if you break a window you have to own up to it and be willing

61

to take the punishment for it," he explained.

"Very good, son." She stood, placed the book in the trunk and locked it once again. "Let's go to my classroom, I want to give you something."

Jerry followed her up the stairs and into her classroom. He looked around at the room with a wooden floor, desks, and a row of tall windows. He looked over the blackboards, stacks of books on a long table in the back, and pictures the students had drawn and hung on the walls. He realized he would not be returning to this cozy place he had called home for over nine months. He actually felt a touch of sadness.

She went to her desk and opened the bottom drawer where she pulled out a piece of paper rolled up with a red ribbon around it. Jerry moved closer and she slid the ribbon off and unrolled the document-like paper. "Jerry, this is something I had printed many years ago when I realized my calling in life was to help young people make this world a better place for others. I vowed I would give it to those students I believed would make a great impact on society."

She handed the paper to him. It was titled THE CREED, and read: This Certificate is Given to Master Jerry Watson (his name had been written in the blank), For Outstanding Achievement in Mrs. Richardson's Sixth Grade Class. It was inscribed with the following principles: Have Faith in God; Get an Education, Work Hard; and Take Personal Responsibility for Your Actions. It was dated and signed, Mrs. Richardson, Sixth Grade Teacher.

"Thank you." Jerry hugged her for the last time and ran out the door. He could not explain his feelings, but he knew something special had just happened. He thought he heard a voice say, "Jerry, this is a turning point for you. The information you received today will change your life." ...

"Ouch!" The high pitched scream came from the tent. "I'm gonna tell mama." The small boy darted out from under the quilts and was running as fast as his little legs would carry him toward the store. "Mammmmmaaaa!"

Jerry snapped back to the scene in the yard. "Hey little fella, what happened?"

The little boy suddenly stopped in front of Jerry, tears streaked down dirt caked cheeks. He stared at the tall man dressed in jeans and an Atlanta Braves shirt. "Buster's been hittin' me on the head and I'm gonna tell mama," he cried and bolted through the screen door.

Jerry watched the door bounce a couple of times and rest unevenly against the frame. He walked around to the side of the store past the air compressor and to the front where the gas pumps were located. The old lady was fueling an older but immaculate Chevy Belair.

6

"Son, don't you value your life?" the smartly dressed owner of the Lincoln Mark IV had returned from the rest room and was standing beside Jerry.

"Huh?" Jerry cocked his head and blew out a long stream of bluish smoke into the air.

Irritated he blurted. "Don't you realize you could ignite those fumes and blow us all up?"

"Naw, I don't place too much value on it." Jerry said arrogantly, as he finished pumping the gas and took out the nozzle. "Do you want your oil checked?"

"No I don't, young man, here's my credit card, I've got an appointment to make, so hurry it up."

Jerry finished with the customer and sat down on a wooden bench in front of Malone's Sinclair Service Station. Jeff Malone had given him a job when he was only fourteen, and now that he was seventeen and a high school dropout, it was even more important to have a job. It kept him in wheels, though it was not much, his '62 Ford Fairlane got him around town. He also had a little money left over to buy cigarettes and go out on the weekends when he was not working. The rest of his money went to his older brother Dale who let him live in a little sharecropper house he rented about a mile outside of Washburn. Jerry had had enough of Charlie's ranting and raving, especially after Jerry had proved his words were true—"You're never gonna amount to nothin'." The place was small but neither Jerry nor Dale was there enough to get in one another's way. Dale was working at the local plywood mill and Jerry spent most of his time at Malone's.

Jerry was puffing on another Marlboro when he looked up and saw Mrs. Richardson driving up in her shiny new Buick. He jumped up and wiped his hands on an oily rag and headed back to the pumps. His stomach knotted up as she pulled in front of the first pump and got out of her car with her usual broad smile. "Hi Jerry, how are you son?"

"Fine, thank you. What will it be?"

"Fill it up, please." She walked around the car and stood near Jerry. He knew what she was going to say before she said it—*Jerry you're too smart to spend your life working at a gas station. Go back to school and get an education. You can do something special with your life.*

"Jerry?"

"Yes ma'am," Jerry put the nozzle in the tank and began dispensing the gas.

"Son, you are too smart to waste your life pumping gas. You need to go back to school and get an education. God wants to do something special in your life."

"Yes ma'am," he uttered his usual reply. He finished pumping the gas and noted that it took only four gallons. "Why does she do this?" He wanted to tell her to leave him alone, but he had too much respect for her. And then there was that faint desire to become a lawyer, her visits gave him encouragement that he could accomplish something with his life.

"Jerry, remember The Creed?" were her final words as she drove away.

The Creed! Sure, he remembered it, somewhere in the deep recesses of his mind the simple principles she shared that day in the basement, and the words written on the scroll. It had only been five years, but somehow that all seemed a long time ago. He spit on the ground and headed to the cash register. ...

The pounding on the front door startled Jerry from a sound sleep. "Hey boys! Wake up in there." The deep voice boomed into the blackness of the night. Jerry reached over and turned on the lamp near his bed and looked at the alarm clock–it was 2:30. Thump, thump, thump! "Hey boys! Wake up. It's Sheriff Scott."

By then Dale was stumbling down the hall pulling on his pants. "We're coming," he yelled. Jerry leaped out of bed and met him as he reached for the door knob. He turned the knob and simultaneously turned on the porch light. Sheriff Waymon Scott, tall and lanky, stood on the small front porch with two of his deputies. Jerry knew these men well, he took care of their squad cars because the county bought their gas from Jeff's. Their somber looks gave Jerry a queasy feeling. Something was not right and he immediately thought of his mother and the abuse she had taken over the years from Charlie. Jerry had told him when he left home that if he ever touched her again he was going to kill him. "Had he hit her again?" Jerry wondered.

"What's the matter Sheriff?" Dale was the first to speak up.

"I'm afraid I got some bad news for you boys," the older man said. "Your step-daddy, Charlie Watson, was killed tonight."

"What? How? What's going on. Is my mother okay?" Dale was firing questions at him. Jerry's bare feet were frozen to the wood floor, his mouth open.   He instantly saw Charlie with the meat cleaver in his back that his mama used to hack away at meat in their grocery store. Then he saw him laying dead with a bullet in his head on the little trail behind Lester's house, a bottle of whiskey at his side.   And finally he saw him slumped over in his Chevy truck as its twisted frame rested against a pine tree on one of the dirt roads near his house.

"Just settle down son." Sheriff Scott reached out and placed his hand on Dale's shoulder. "I'll tell you all I know. It happened over in Lowndes County so I don't have all the facts, but it seems he was at a juke joint over there tonight. After a few too many he went home with some old gal."

"Did she kill him?" Jerry was surprised to hear himself ask.

The Sheriff turned to Jerry and said, "No Jerry, her husband did. He's been arrested, but I don't know if they're gonna be able to hold him."

Jerry had heard enough, he turned and went back to the cot in the living room where he slept. He had pretty much expected Charlie would meet his end like that. He did not feel anything for Charlie, but he worried about his mama. What would she do now? No husband–no money. He fell on the cot and stared into the alarm clock, it was 2:38. The man who had told him so many times that he would never amount to anything was dead.

"Okay Sheriff, we're heading over to see our mother right now," he heard his brother say.

The funeral was simple and it was short. There was not much the preacher could say. Charlie had rarely gone to church and his opinion of preachers and Christians was always critical, if not hostile. A handful of people were present: Virgil and a few of the other regulars at Last Stop. When

68

it was over the family filed out first, the four boys surrounded their mother and comforted her as best they could. It was difficult for Jerry for he hated the man who abused him and his mother. The February wind was blustery and clouds were forming in the sky when they stepped outside and into the limousine which would take them to the cemetery. By the time they reached the final resting place the heavens opened and the rains descended. Only the immediate family stood over the casket as it was lowered into the ground.

After Charlie's funeral Jerry moved back in with his mother. At first he stayed close to home, but before long he was hanging out with the guys again. ...

"Look out!" The burly boy called Burt yelled and jumped off the side of the bank. The gigantic wave nearly sunk Jerry.

"Bombs away!" another boy made a canon ball and hit the water near Jerry and the force of the waves rocked him back and forth. This time Jerry went under and gulped the icy spring water. The beers he drank earlier began to affect him and he fairly struggled to keep his head above water. Then his best friend George came in like a torpedo and he sank again. Finally Jerry gained his equilibrium and reached for a limb on the bank and pulled himself out of the water.

"What's the matter, Jerry, can't you take a little fun?" the tall red headed boy named Ricky called.

He crawled onto the bank, gasping for air and coughing up spoonfuls of water. Clearing his lungs and throat, he grunted. "Listen, at one o'clock in the morning, after about a case of beer, and in the coldest springs in Whitley County, I think I got the

69

right to cough up some water," Jerry defended himself.

Burt laughed. "Okay, Slick. I guess you do have the right to lay out for a while. But I'm bored, and since we didn't kill anybody here tonight, I propose we go do something exciting, like rob the bank."

"Ha ha," Brian, a short stocky boy, laughed. "What makes you think we can get by Barney. He'll put us all in jail."

The other boys burst out with another cackle.

"You mean Fred Barney Fife, the best darned deputy in Whitley County." George roared with laughter and the others joined him.

Fred Beasley was the lone policeman for Washburn. He was skinny, had poor sight and seemed confused a great deal of the time. Most town folks believed he had the job only because his brother-in-law was on the city council. The young people made fun of him and called him Barney because he reminded them of the inept deputy on the popular Andy Griffith Show."

"Ah, don't bother old Barney. He's probably just settling in for his regular nap." Jerry pulled himself up beside his brother's blue and white '55 Chevy and lit a Marlboro.

"Hey Jerry! Remember the time we siphoned gas out of old man Sullivan's pick up truck while he was drunk on the side the road and old Barney drove by three times and never caught us?" Ricky Jackson chimed in.

"Yea." Jerry blew smoke out of the side of his mouth and leaned over the warm Chevy hood to dry out his wet body. "He sure was four eyes that night, he couldn't see what was going on right in front of him." The boys roared again with laughter and made their way to Burt's pick up and tore the top off of a Styrofoam ice chest filled with beer.

"Well, whadaya say?" Burt asked no one in particular.

"What do you say about what?" Jerry asked. The moon was full and the water oaks cast spooky looking shadows as the moon cascaded through them.

"Last one outta here is a chicken," Burt shouted. The boys scrambled for the vehicles. Jerry and George jumped in the '55 Chevy while Burt dove behind the wheel of his daddy's green International truck with Brian and Ricky in the back.

Jerry started his car first, roared the engine, and slammed the transmission into drive. The tires kicked up sand and grass as he sped toward the narrow opening between crepe myrtle trees and out into the graded road that led to town. Burt was right behind him as he burst through the opening and yanked the steering wheel to the left and gunned it on the straight of way. George lurched toward the driver as he grabbed onto the door handle to hold on.

"Look at that idiot!" George exclaimed. The old International loomed large in the rear view mirror.

"Whoa baby!" Jerry called out. He whipped the truck to the right and fish tailed around a hair pin turn. George went crashing into the door.

"Man, look at those guys eating dust." George righted himself, turned sideways and reached for the dash board as he looked back at Burt coughing and fanning dust out of his cab. The two boys in the back of the truck were holding on for dear life. "Look out! He's trying to pass."

Jerry clutched the wheel tighter, hunched over it, and suddenly steered sharply to the left to cut Burt off. Burt veered toward the ditch but snatched it back just in time. Jerry could hear him let loose a string of curse words as he decelerated and tailgated the Chevy.

"I hope nobody's on this road tonight, cause if they are they're gonna get killed." George had learned to hang on and view the race with delight.

Finally they came to a paved county road and Jerry slammed on brakes. Burt skidded to within inches of Jerry's bumper, leaving deep skid marks in the dirt road. Jerry left his motor running and ran back to Burt's truck and grabbed onto the side view mirror. "Hey! We beat ya." Jerry bragged.

"Aw, you ain't done nothin'." Burt leaped out of the truck, spit a long stream of brownish chewing tobacco on the ground and slapped the hood of his truck. "This is kid's stuff. Now, why don't we do something that's a real challenge. I suggest we go down to Four Oaks Cafe and see how much cash they left in the register tonight. And besides, we need to give old Barney a test."

"What do you mean?" Jerry wanted to know.

"I mean, Slick, that we break in and take the cash." Burt moved closer to Jerry and stood in front of him. "What do you say? Do you want to do it, or are you chicken?"

Jerry tried to swallow without the other boys seeing. His palms became sweaty and he felt his heart pounding so loud he was afraid Burt could hear it. "I don't have to break the law to prove I'm tough."

"That's right, buddy." Burt ejected another stream of tobacco onto the ground. He reached down and tapped the smaller boy on the chest. "But I dare you."

"Come on Jerry. You're not afraid are you?" Ricky asked.

Jerry looked around nervously at the other boys. His stomach knotted up and he felt beads of sweat dripping down the small of his back. It felt like the time he was in the Little League batting line up. His team was facing the fastest and wildest pitcher in the league. The previous batter had been hit and when Jerry did not step up to the plate his coach came over to find out why. Jerry said he was sick to his stomach, but really it was fear that paralyzed him. But this time he was not going to back down. ...

"Hey, George! Put that cigarette out," Jerry whispered back to the boy crouched with him behind the low wall running along the rear of Four Oaks Cafe. The little restaurant was situated right next door to a gas station, with a small pond on one side and several houses just beyond the wall. Low hanging bushes gave the boys some covering. Burt was leading the way and would occasionally stop and look back to see if the others were following.

"When we get to the back door, Jerry I want you to use that crow bar and start to work on the lock," Burt ordered. "George, you take a post behind that car over there and watch the front. Ricky, you go around the east side and watch Highway 56 for any traffic. Brian, you stay here and watch these houses back here. If you see a light come on you whistle and the plan's off. Get it?"

"Yeah," the boys chorused.

Jerry thought he heard Mrs. Richardson's voice saying, "Don't do it son." But he had come too far, and besides, if they were successful he would be held in high esteem by somebody, even if it was just Burt and the guys. Soon the boys were in position. Jerry and Burt were at the back door with the crow bar.

"I can't get the end of this thing behind the lock," Jerry grunted. With each try the crow slipped.

"Let me try it." Burt pushed the smaller boy out of the way and grabbed the bar. "You gotta put some muscle in it Slick." The big boy poked the bar between the jam and the door and heaved against it until there was a popping sound and the door flew open. Burt grabbed it quickly and pulled it shut to keep the light from shining outdoors. He looked around nervously. "Do you see anybody?"

"No." Jerry surveyed the area and saw Mrs. People's house right behind the cafe was still dark and quiet. The two other houses were also peaceful except for a street light which lit up the front yards. There were no cars on the street either.

"Okay, let's go." Burt opened the door slightly and slipped through the small opening with Jerry following. Burt knew the lay out of the cafe well since he had worked in it for three straight summers. He went directly to the NCR cash register and opened it with a couple of punches and a pull of the handle. "Doggone it. They took all the money out."

Jerry followed and watched the angry boy slam the door shut with a thud. He proceeded to a back room and Jerry stayed out front and looked through the plate glass windows to the street beyond. He was thinking about Mr. and Mrs. Owens who owned the cafe. They were decent people and he wished he was not violating their property. He looked around at the modest dining room with wooden tables, red and white checkered table cloths, and chairs still turned upside down on the tables. The Owens' cleaned the place themselves because they could not afford help. It was the only cafe in town but the Owens' did not charge the same as the big city restaurants and profits were low. Jerry felt a sense of shame and spoke out, "I'm getting out of here Burt. This ain't right."

Suddenly Burt appeared from the back room cursing. "It ain't there. The money box is missing."

"I'm leaving," Jerry repeated and turned to go. "I don't want any part of this."

"So you're gonna chicken out on me, are you?" Burt glared at him.

"Call it what you want, I'm leaving," he called over his shoulder as he was half way out the dining area and in the stock room. Burt followed protesting. When he reached the back door the other boys were waiting on them. "I'm leaving guys. The Owens' haven't done anything to me and I'm not gonna hurt them."

Just then car lights flooded the spot where the boys were congregated and a man yelled. "Police!" It was Fred Beasley. "Stay where you are and put your hands up."

Jerry froze in his tracks but Burt and the other boys bolted. "It's just old Barney," Burt laughed as he and the others ran toward Ricky's house where they had left their trucks. Jerry did not move and was determined he was going to stay and face the music.

When Deputy Beasley saw the other boys flee he scrambled back to his squad car and raced down Second Street, lights flashing. The four boys had beaten a path through the neighbor's yards and arrived at Ricky's house before the deputy. The green International peeled rubber as they sped down Scranton Street on their way out of town. Jerry stood in the moonlight behind the cafe. He saw lights come on in all three houses situated behind it. Momentarily Mr. Otterman appeared, buttoning his shirt as he stepped on his back porch.

He and Jerry looked toward Ricky's house but

neither was able to see anything. They heard tires peeling, engines roaring, and yells. Jerry recognized the deep throttle of Burt's dad's International as it headed from Scranton Street and toward Cross Creek road. He heard the low hanging bumper make an eerie shriek as it scraped the pavement when the big truck bounced up and banged down at the Seaboard Coast Line Railroad crossing. He also heard the long, piercing whistle of the early morning freight train hauling coal from the West Virginia mines to the big Florida power companies. It was always on time, and because it came through at approximately 2:00 a. m., it hardly slowed for the little town of Washburn. Again Jerry heard the train whistle ring out long and loud, then the squad car's siren, the roaring engines, tires squealing, and then Jerry was stunned as he heard something too incredible to believe—a sickening crunch preceded by a long and sustained blast of the train whistle. At that moment Mr. Otterman looked in Jerry's direction and the two of them locked in a cold, icy stare. ...

"Mr. Jerry! Are you all right?" Caleb asked anxiously.

"Huh?" Jerry shook his head. He was ashen white and was sweating profusely. He recognized the hitchhiker he had picked up just a couple of hours earlier standing beside him under the carport of the country store.

"You have an awful pained looked on your face, Mr. Jerry. Is everything all right? Do you want to talk to me about it?"

The old lady from the store came hurriedly out the front door with a small bottle of Coca Cola in her hand, "Here!" she said and thrust it at Jerry.

7

"Mr. Jerry! Are you okay? Caleb tugged at his sleeve. "Here. Take this and drink it. You look like you have seen an apparition."

"I think I did, Caleb." Jerry reached for the Coca Cola and took a sip. He wiped perspiration from his brow with the back of his hand and looked up into the noon day sun.

"Do you want to talk about it?" the old man asked again.

Jerry turned and looked into the kind, old face. There was something about his countenance that made him want to tell him the whole story. This fatherly figure exuded a love and concern that had escaped Jerry as a child and he felt as though if he told Caleb everything that he would make it right. Jerry started to talk, but looked around for the old lady.

"She went inside." Caleb threw a thumb toward the store then made a sweeping motion with his right hand. "Let's sit over there in that swing, I'm sure the owner wouldn't mind."

The two men made their way to a cypress porch swing which was attached with chains to a four by four post. The overhead post rested on two posts about six feet apart located in the front yard of the residence under a shady mimosa tree. It was a pleasant setting with rose bushes climbing a trellis, fresh cut grass, a flower bed with Jerry's favorite, elephant ears, and a small fountain in the center. They sat down on the swing and rocked back and forth slowly for a few minutes before Caleb spoke up. "Would you like to talk about it?"

Jerry turned to the man and said, "Who ARE you?"

"I'm just an old man, of no account. All I have to offer you is an ear." He bent over, put his hands together as if he was praying, and touched the tips of his fingers to his lips. "Mr. Jerry, I've traveled many miles and met a lot of people, rich and poor, young and old, educated and uneducated–and they all had problems. I discovered if you give a person a chance to talk about his problems he usually feels better."

"Caleb, I've told you a little about me, but you do not know the whole story. Most people who know me do not know the real Jerry Watson. I graduated from law school and became a very successful lawyer. I have a very responsible position–I'm one of many advisors to the President of the United States. I've got everything money can buy, and not only that, I've got the greatest wife and kids in the world. A year ago, even six months ago, I would have told you that things were going great in my life, but now...." Jerry stopped and breathed deeply, "now, I can't say that. It seems that my whole life has fallen apart." He shifted uneasily in the swing.

"Why don't you tell me about it."

Jerry hesitated for just a moment, then he plunged ahead. "I'm going to tell you some things about myself that my wife Mary Ann doesn't even know. I was born in Washburn, a small town in South Georgia, to Buddy and Lettie Green, they had four boys. My daddy got killed in a farming accident when I was three. My brother Dale was six and the twins, Jeremy and Justin were only six months old. My mama married a man by the name of Charlie Watson, he was well known as a drunk and womanizer. I don't think my mama ever loved him but she married him because she needed help raising four boys. She told me he adopted all four of us, although I don't know why, he abused all of us." Jerry's face drew grim as he thought of his life with Charlie. "Charlie owned a little country store which was a combination grocery store and juke joint. A juke joint is a bar, or saloon, or tavern."

Caleb chuckled, "I have traveled the southern United States many times and understand the colloquialism." He was now sitting with a leg propped under the other and his right arm thrown over the back of the swing. Blue had made his way out of the truck and stood wagging his tail in front of them. Caleb reached down and patted him on his head and as if on cue the dog lay down at their feet.

"Actually, it was a place much like this one, very much like this one." Jerry surveyed the long block building with amazement. "My mama was good to me, but Charlie Watson was mean and he made our lives miserable. As I was growing up he constantly told me I wouldn't amount to anything." Jerry turned to the old man. "Do you know what that can do to a person?"

"I do, Mr. Jerry. I've seen it time and time again. I can't tell you how many men I've met and counseled who were mentally abused by their fathers, told they were no good, that they wouldn't succeed in life. Sadly, the world has no shortage of stories like yours." Caleb lowered his head but popped up quickly. "But you have become a success!"

"When I took a psychology course in college I learned what Charlie had done to me. He had effectively destroyed my self esteem. I thought so

79

little of myself that I wouldn't even go to school. I was embarrassed because I didn't feel like I measured up and as a result I quit school in the tenth grade."

"It's obvious you went back to school and received an excellent education. How did you do that?"

"It didn't happen over night, but as an adult looking back on my life I know that things started to change when I was in the sixth grade, and specifically because of my teacher, Mrs. Richardson. She planted seeds in my life that eventually produced a harvest."

"Tell me about this Mrs. Richardson."

"Oh Caleb, she was the most wonderful person in the world. She was kind, thoughtful, sensitive, and caring. I fell in love with her, as a twelve year old I wanted to marry her. I was devastated when I found out she had a husband."

"It is not unusual for a twelve year old to have a crush on his teacher."

"It was more than a crush! Mrs. Richardson gave me hope, she believed in me, and her confidence in me eventually helped me believe in myself."

"Is this Mrs. Richardson still alive?" Caleb inquired.

"Yes, as a matter of fact she is. She lives in a nursing home in Washburn. I have not seen her in many years. She must be in her eighties now." Jerry sat back in the swing and became more relaxed as he shared some of the more pleasant memories of his past. "I still send her flowers on her birthday and drop her a note every once in a while to update her on what one of her students is doing. She can't write for herself but I receive correspondence from the nurses who tell me they appreciate my staying in touch."

"She must have been very special to you."

"She was, Caleb. Without her instruction and encouragement I can say I would not be where I am today." Jerry leaned forward and used his hands to communicate. "She instilled in me The Creed."

"What's that?"

"Four simple but dynamic principles the pilgrims followed when they founded and developed this great country of ours. Those who have followed The Creed have experienced success and prosperity beyond their wildest dreams. It has made this country the greatest economic power on the face of the earth. As Mrs. Richardson explained it to me Caleb, the Pilgrims left everything–their homes, lands, and their families and risked their lives to begin a new life. They had very little with which to start over, and many died pursuing their dream."

"I'm anxious to hear about these principles."

"Well, as I said, they are simple, but if they are put into use they are very powerful. The four principles are: Have Faith in God; Get an Education; Work Hard; and Take Personal Responsibility for Your Life." Jerry looked at Caleb. "That's it! That's The Creed that Mrs. Richardson taught me in sixth grade."

"Wow! Are those the principles you used to achieve the great success you have had?"

"I'm sorry to say I didn't employ these principles until almost ten years later, after I had suffered so much."

"Did you ever tell Mrs. Richardson that you attribute much of your success to her teachings and encouragement?"

"As a matter of fact I never did. After I quit school I went to work at a gas station, bought a car, and hung out with all the other guys in town. I was headed nowhere, though there were seeds of greatness planted in me. I sensed something extraordinary in me."

"What happened to make you see the light?"

"When I was seventeen I was hanging out with the rest of the guys who were going nowhere. We had just finished drinking and horsing around at Roy Springs, when one of the guys dared us to break into a local cafe and steal their cash. At first I agreed, and I did in fact break in the place, but once inside I changed my mind. I couldn't stand the thought of doing something so terrible to decent people. It was uncanny, but I thought I heard Mrs. Richardson's voice tell me I should not do it. I think The Creed was beginning to take effect. Just about the time I told Burt I was not going through with the burglary a policeman arrived and the other guys fled. I stayed behind. There was a high speed chase and a policeman was killed. All of us were charged with second degree murder under the state's felony murder doctrine."

"My goodness!" For the first time Caleb seemed genuinely shocked. "What happened?"

"I went to court, and I will tell you it was the worst experience of my life, that is up until the last several weeks." Jerry looked drained as he relived the terrible experience. "I was tried and found guilty of a lesser offense. Because I confessed, and had others corroborate my story that I had changed my mind, the judge was lenient. Several people spoke on my behalf, including Mrs. Richardson. And even the Owens', who owned the cafe, tearfully asked the judge to go easy on me citing my hard upbringing. The fact that it was my first offense helped also. But I still had to serve time at a minimum security prison in North Georgia."

"It must have been hard for a young man who was rejected by his father to serve time in prison."

"It sounds strange, but prison actually helped me. Don't misunderstand..." Jerry held up his hand. "I'm not saying bad things should happen to you to get your attention, but when something tragic occurs we can use it as a stepping stone. Prison life helped discipline me. And I had the time to think about what I wanted to do with my life."

"It sounds like you learned some valuable lessons in prison."

"Well, I wouldn't say I learned them as much as I began to believe in the things I was taught as a boy, especially The Creed."

"Did Mrs. Richardson visit you in prison?"

"Absolutely!" Jerry smiled broadly. "She was there every month encouraging me. She told me I could use the unfortunate event to turn my life around. At first I didn't want to hear that, but after a while I warmed up to the idea and we developed that closeness that we had when I was in sixth grade. She continued to preach the four principles of The Creed–Have Faith in God, Get an Education, Work Hard and Take Personal Responsibility for Your Life."

"Did you follow those precepts?"

"Yes I did. I worked on the prison farm. I asked for that job because some of the few good memories I have of my childhood were of helping my grandpa Bell on his farm. I was up at 5:30 every morning. We had hogs and cows to feed, and crops such as millet, corn, watermelons, and tobacco to plant, cultivate, and harvest. It was hard work, in the hot sun, but it was good for me. It instilled in me a work ethic that I would employ in law school and in my practice that would serve me well and help me succeed."

"Did you come to grips with your responsibility for the crime?"

"Yes, I did. Mrs. Richardson always stressed personal responsibility as one of the central themes of The Creed, without it she said everything else would fail. She said, 'God gave every man the freedom to choose. He can choose to do right, or he can choose to do wrong, and when he suffers the consequences of doing wrong, he can't blame God or anyone else for it.' When I finally grasped the fact that I was in prison because of my wrong choices, that it wasn't Burt, or Charlie Watson, or my mama, or anyone else who caused it, then my attitude changed to where I could deal with it positively."

"So you didn't blame your step-father for your predicament. That's admirable Mr. Jerry, most people would have blamed him for such a horrible experience."

"I know, but most people languish in self pity and misery–and I was determined not to do that. I was the one who made the mistake of following Burt to Owens Cafe that night. I couldn't blame it on anybody else." Jerry stood up and stretched his legs. "You know Caleb, when I accepted responsibility for my crime it was the most liberating experience of my life. If I caused the mess, then I could do something about getting out."

"As I've traveled this great nation of yours, I've discovered people are less and less willing to accept responsibility for their actions. They blame it on everybody from their parents, to their teachers, to the government." Caleb sighed.

Jerry wondered what he meant by *this nation of yours*, but said nothing. He was indeed feeling better about getting his secretive past off of his chest. He sat down in the swing once again and the two men rocked it slowly back and forth.

"What about the principle of getting an education, certainly you heeded it well, but how did you do it?"

"As I said, Mrs. Richardson visited me every month, and she would bring her books with her. She had been assigned by the school board to head up adult education for the summer and part of her job was to help adults pass the GED test. I wasn't eligible to take the test until I was eighteen, but since that was just a few months away, she had me sign up for a study program. It wasn't long before I had a General Equivalency Diploma which I proudly display today."

"But isn't it a long way from a General Equivalency Diploma to Law School, especially one as distinguished as Duke?"

"It certainly is, but I learned that if you are determined and persevere you can accomplish just about anything you want to do. Once I received the diploma I found out I could take courses through a local community college while I was in prison. I took Western Civilization and English I and made an A in both courses. My college career had begun." Jerry leaned back and seemed revived once again as he rehearsed his victories. He put the small coke bottle to his mouth and took another swig. "I was released on good behavior within the year and I enrolled as a full time student. I studied hard and made all A's in community college. I applied to the University of Georgia and was accepted. Thankfully I finished college with the financial help of Mrs. Richardson and various part time jobs. I continued to do well at the university and, when I made an outstanding score on the Law School Aptitude Test, it opened up a scholarship for me at Duke University Law School. But to answer your question—after I became a success, I never got a chance to sit down with Mrs. Richardson and tell her how much she meant to me. I have sent her money but I haven't been back to Washburn since I left that day in the deputy sheriff's car with a pair of handcuffs on my wrists."

"Mr. Jerry, you told me that your wife doesn't know about some of your past," said Caleb, who being fully revived, leaned close to Jerry.

"Mary Ann," Jerry whispered her name. "Mary Ann. She is the most beautiful person in my world Caleb and easily the most important one in my life. I dare say, I would never have attained such success if it wasn't for that woman."

"She is that important, yet you never told her about your past?"

"Oh, she knows a lot of my past, but she doesn't know about prison and about Charlie. She's never been to Washburn and she never asked me about my past—that's one thing I love about her. We met one cool fall day on the campus at Duke University. I was playing quarterback for my law school class intramural football team—we were called the Tortfeasors." Jerry chuckled. "She was dating a guy on the other team and was standing on the sidelines rooting for him. I dropped back to pass and zipped one to my receiver on a down and out pattern. Unfortunately for her, but as it turned out, fortunately for me, I hit her square on the nose. It knocked her out and she had to be carried to the hospital. I visited her several times after that and tried talking her into letting me take her out to make up for it. Reluctantly she agreed. Soon after that we fell madly in love with each other and since then there has been no one but Mary Ann."

"That's a beautiful story book meeting."

"Yes, but I never could muster the courage to tell her about prison. I was afraid she might reject me. After we were married it just didn't seem to matter then."

"But now, does it matter now?" The old man suddenly looked sad again.

"I think so—yes.... I don't know." Jerry lowered his head, and slowly shook it as he rested it in his hands. "Caleb, I've always been in control of my life and circumstances, but things have gotten away from me and I must admit I am scared. I don't know what to do."

"I assume this information has not been made available to the President or to his advisors."

" I wasn't required to go through a confirmation process but the FBI did do a cursory check of my background. I tried to tell them the whole story but they were in such a hurry to confirm top level cabinet positions that my appointment didn't seem that important to them. Besides, they seemed too confident that I would have no problem being approved since I had already been working with the staff on the campaign. Also, my criminal record had been expunged, but it didn't erase the fact that it had happened. The problem now is that CNN has picked up on the information and is prepared to use it to humiliate the president."

"And your president has been through quite a bit lately?" Caleb broke in. "I seem to recall it started when he nominated a very wealthy businessman to be Secretary of the Interior who, it was later learned, had a criminal background. It was quite an embarrassment for the President. Then there was the lady who was nominated as Attorney General who withdrew her name because she had had an affair. Not to mention all the problems with the anti-Castro group and grid lock and religion and all the other issues that contributed to the pressures you find yourself under today. It doesn't look very good for you, does it?"

"Caleb I think you have a pretty good understanding of the problems."

"Mr. Jerry?" the old man looked at him with sad eyes.

"Yes, Caleb?" Jerry felt bonded with this stranger.

"Do you realize you haven't said anything about the principle—Have Faith in God?"

"I didn't mean to leave it out. It has certainly been important to me. I believe there is a God, and He definitely helped me make it through so many difficult times of my life. I attended chapel in prison, read the Bible frequently, and prayed fairly often. I absolutely believe that principle is very important, and my wife Mary Ann is a devout Christian."

"You said you feel like something is missing in your life, that you've followed the principles but something is not quite right."

"I don't remember saying that to you Caleb."

"Is it true?"

"Yes, it is true. But I can't put my finger on what it is. I just feel that it is very important and I must find out what it is."

"Mr. Jerry, I believe your answer is waiting for you in Washburn."

"Washburn?"

"I don't think you have grasped all that The Creed entails, and who is best able to teach you?" the old man asked.

"Mrs. Richardson!?" Jerry blurted out

incredulously.

"I think you must go and see her."

"I haven't talked with her in over twenty five years. What could she possibly say that would be any different than what she told me then?" Jerry was puzzled.

Caleb suddenly jumped up and pointed his long finger south. "You must go to Washburn and see Mrs. Richardson!" he shouted.

8

Jerry swung the truck onto the road and looked into his rear view mirror at the old lady standing under the carport with a broom in her hand. As they pulled away from the little country store she offered a feeble wave of the hand and then began to sweep the concrete floor. Blue was curled up against the tail gate and Caleb sat motionless in the passenger seat. He had a distant look on his face as he peered through the windshield. Before they had traveled a mile a thunderstorm suddenly appeared and a deluge ensued. Jerry quickly rolled up his window and checked once again on Blue who was finding some shelter under the tent. "Where in the world did this storm come from?"

Caleb did not seem to hear his question. "Turn here and it will take you back to I-20." He commanded.

"How do you know that?"

"Mr. Jerry, there's no time to explain, just do as I say. We must get to Washburn before dark." There was an urgency in his voice that had not been there before.

Jerry slowed the truck to a near stop and hung over the steering wheel and tried to follow the barely visible yellow line of the road. He wished he had not left the security of the store, but it was impossible to turn around and go back. He felt an odd foreboding, an oppression, as the wind howled and the rain came down in torrents. For the first time in a long while Jerry was afraid for his safety.

"You must hurry Mr. Jerry." The old man had slouched over and placed his fingers together and touched them to his lips.

"Now wait a minute!" Jerry exclaimed, eyes darting toward the intense man. "I'm not going to speed and risk our lives. I don't see the necessity of having to get to Washburn before dark, or at any time for that matter. I think it is time you told me who you are and what you are doing here!"

Caleb turned to him with the big beautiful eyes that seemed to be pools of love and compassion. The warm peaceful feeling Jerry had experienced when he first met him rushed through him once again. "Mr. Jerry!" he pleaded, tears filling his eyes. "Please don't ask any more questions, just keep going. This storm will pass, but there will be other obstacles." He turned back to the windshield and squinted as he looked beyond the storm.

The sound of his voice calmed Jerry and he was unable to press the issue. He turned back to the wheel and pushed down on the accelerator. He could not explain why, but he felt that they would be safe. Then, just as quickly as the skies got dark and the storm grew worse, it stopped. The clouds broke, the wind ceased, and the sun shined through.

"Look!" Jerry pointed ahead. "It's I-20." He increased his speed and made his way to the entrance ramp and onto the interstate. Shortly he was up to maximum speed and cruising eastward.

Caleb relaxed a bit but remained aloof. He appeared to be in deep thought, or even in prayer. It was now after 2:00 o'clock in the afternoon. Jerry calculated that they would reach Washburn before 7:00 p. m. If indeed there was a reason to get there before dark, they should make it. Jerry looked at

Caleb again and saw his eyes were closed, but his lips moved slightly. He was puzzled at his change of demeanor. He was not the same relaxed man he had picked up just a few hours earlier. He looked once again in the mirror and saw Blue standing in the center of the truck bed shaking himself vigorously and allowing the wind to dry him.

The quietness of the time gave Jerry a chance to reflect on the unusual events which had taken place that morning. He was not sure if he had dreamed what had happened or if it actually occurred. He thought about Mary Ann and the kids. The last thing she said to him before he kissed her and walked out of the bedroom at 6:30 was, "I love you, Honey, and I'm praying for you."

Jerry shook his head and, realizing he was heading back to Atlanta, his anxiety level rose. He reached over and pulled out a map from the glove compartment. Caleb was now asleep and he was careful so as not to disturb him. Jerry took the map and held it against the steering wheel while he drove. He spotted the highway he was looking for and decided that he would take it south and pick up I-75 to south Georgia and the little town where he was born. "No need to get too close to Atlanta and be reminded of what I left at the office," he whispered.

After a few minutes on I-20 the silence was too much for Jerry and he turned on the radio. The original Delco stereo system sounded as good as when Jerry listened to it in the early 70s. The Golden Oldie station out of Atlanta was playing one of his favorites, "Can't Take My Eyes Off You" by the Four Seasons. The high pitched sound of Frankie Valli's voice pierced the silent cab and Caleb stirred just a bit. The song ended and a deep male voice boomed, "This is a WFOX newsbreak.

Good afternoon everyone this is Sandy Stoneman. Braves fans will be happy to know that America's team will be opening its home schedule at Turner Field in Atlanta in just two short weeks. In other news, President Kenneth Morton is traveling in South America to highlight his administration's support of the North/South Free Trade Agreement. An administration spokesman said the President will be making some changes in his staff, which includes advisors, and higher ups in the White House. Recent scandals and inability to uncork the economy has been troubling to the President who faces a tough reelection year. And now ...."

Jerry lurched forward and turned off the radio. The news made the sick feeling return to his stomach. He looked at the map again and wished that he could start heading south instead of toward Atlanta. Caleb was still asleep and Blue had settled down in the back of the truck. Then he looked up saw and his exit. He glanced in his rear view mirror and noticed a large, semi-truck approaching rapidly in his lane. He did not think much about it until the dusty vehicle came within inches of his truck, then whipped into the left lane. "Wow!" Jerry exclaimed. "That guy just missed me."

Suddenly the sixteen wheeler veered into Jerry's lane, forcing him to hit the emergency lane. "Hey!" Jerry called out louder. "You're gonna kill us." Then the big truck swerved back into the left lane.

Caleb's head popped up from where it had been resting on his chin and his eyes were wild with excitement. "Look out!" he cried. The big Mack truck swung once again into Jerry's lane and forced him into the emergency lane again. As the truck swung back into its lane Jerry tried to get a look at the driver but the windows were too dirty.

Just when he thought the semi was under control he made another lunge at the pick up. This time Jerry had to straddle the ditch and emergency lane to avoid being hit. The grass was wet from the fresh rain and Jerry lost control and began to slide sideways in the ditch.

"Hold on!" Jerry grasped the wheel tighter and held his breath.

"Watch that bridge!" Caleb yelled and grabbed onto the dash board.

Jerry looked and saw a bridge abutment about three hundred feet ahead looming larger. The Mack truck was speeding ahead having taken over the right hand lane. "There's nothing I can do," Jerry yelled. He caught a glimpse of Blue pressed against the side bed of the truck. The tent and other equipment were upside down and scattered in the bed.

"God help us!" Caleb called out. At that moment Jerry righted the truck and whipped it back onto the highway.

"It looked like that guy did that on purpose," Jerry complained once he had the truck under control.

"Mr. Jerry!" Caleb was now fully alert. "How far are we from our destination?"

"Oh, about four hours or so if we stop for gas and something to eat." Jerry looked at his watch.

"I suggest we make no unnecessary stops." Caleb had moved forward once again and was glancing out the window as if he were looking for the enemy. "And please, be watchful."

"Wait a minute." Jerry demanded. "You said you were going west. What happened to that idea?"

Caleb looked drawn as he turned to Jerry, a pitiful sound came out of his mouth. "Mr. Jerry. I am under great stress at this moment. If you believe

I am an honorable gentleman then I ask you to indulge me by allowing me to ride with you to Washburn. Isn't it possible that my plans could have changed after I heard your story? Won't you allow me to be a part of solving your problem?"

Caleb turned back to the windshield once again and began moving his lips. He was fixed and appeared immovable. Jerry decided it was fruitless to continue.

Once again the engine of the 1970 Ford F100 was was humming along a two lane highway. It was 5 p. m. and Jerry noticed the gas gauge was near empty. They were about eighty miles from Washburn. He looked at the old man, who looked older and pale, slumped over against the door asleep. At that time a sign appeared which advertised gas and pecans 5 miles ahead.

Jerry came to a crossroads where there were two stations located. One consisted of a small white building with the sides painted advertising Pecans, Shelled Pecans, Pecan Logs and Gas Cheap. It boasted a lime rock driveway. Two gas pumps out front offered unleaded and premium. There was a young man about twenty-five years old wearing jeans and an army jacket sitting on a bicycle against one of the gas pumps. He looked intently at Jerry, his long brown hair fell over his shoulders and a cigarette hung from his lips. Across the street on the southeast corner was a modern Texaco station with a dozen pumps, a deli, and a food store. Jerry did not hesitate and turned into the Texaco station. The truck bumped as it reached the concrete pavement and it jostled Caleb awake. Even old Blue moved a little and raised up his head.

"We are going to stop and get some gas here," Jerry informed Caleb. "We're a little over an hour from Washburn so I suggest we get something to eat in the deli."

The old man looked through the windshield and observed. "It looks like we're going to make it before dark. But we must hurry, there is no time to waste." He nervously surveyed the area.

"I don't know why you think we have to get to Washburn before dark. But I don't guess it will do any good to ask, so just forget it." He reached in his pocket and pulled out a couple of twenty dollar bills and pushed them toward Caleb. "Here! Go and pay for the gas, and get us a couple of sandwiches and drinks. And get Blue one too."

Caleb took the money and quickly exited the truck and headed to the store.

Jerry jumped out of the truck and called to Blue and patted his head. "Good boy. We're going to get you something to eat."

Jerry took off the gas lid, reached for the handle and pumped the petroleum into the truck. Whenever he visited one of the self-serve stations, he never ceased to think about the many hours he spent at Jeff's Texaco pumping gas for a living. His pulse quickened a bit and he felt butterflies as he thought about the fact that in less than two hours he would be back in the small town that held so many memories for him, a place he had not visited in over two decades.

The pump clicked off and Jerry topped off the tank. He withdrew the nozzle and placed it in the machine. As he turned to put the lid back on he looked up and saw Caleb walking in his direction with two bags. His face suddenly turned ashen, he dropped the bags and began to run toward the truck. He pointed behind Jerry and yelled, "Look out!"

Just then Jerry turned to see the young man he had seen earlier at the other station lunge at him. "Give me your money!" The boy shouted and lifted a knife high over his head and plunged it downward. Jerry managed to throw up his hand and block the thrust of the blade before it connected. The young man was heavier than Jerry and the weight of his body threw him against the truck. As Jerry tried to get up the stranger raised the knife once again. But Jerry knew he was off balance and was powerless to stop the attack. His life briefly flashed before him. It seemed silly but all he could think about was what a miserable death he was about to suffer. Somehow he thought, due to his position and importance, that he should die a more dignified death.

Just as the blade was making it's downward path, Jerry saw a black blur pass in front of him. It was Blue! He let out a fierce growl and crashed into the man and both sprawled on the concrete near the truck. The knife flew out of the young man's hand and glanced off the pavement and into the ditch. By that time Caleb had reached the truck and was hollering at the top of his lungs. "Get out of here! In the Name of the Most High I command you to get out of here!"

Blue was growling and ripping at the man's sleeve but he managed to get to his feet and ran as fast as he could with Blue nipping at his heels. Jerry jumped to his feet and dusted himself off while Caleb grabbed his arm and said, "Let's go Mr. Jerry! Let's go now!"

"Okay, okay! We'll go after him, but first I am going to call the police."

"No! No! Mr. Jerry." Caleb sounded desperate. "We must go to Washburn now."

"What do you mean?" Jerry sounded incredulous. "That guy tried to kill me. I am not going to let him get away with...."

"I said, let's go!" Caleb looked at Jerry with

steel cold eyes. "We do not have time to waste on someone of so little significance. You have more important matters to deal with."

Jerry was stunned more by Caleb's authoritative words than by the attack. There was something so compelling in his voice that he had to obey him. He did not like it that this stranger seemed to have so much power over him, but he could not say no. Caleb pushed him into the cab and ran around to the passenger side and jumped in. Jerry started the truck, revved the motor and peeled rubber as he spun out of the lot. He raced down the road several hundred feet and stopped to pick up Blue who had given up on the chase. The stranger had jumped a fence and fled into dark thick brush.

Jerry was upset for quite awhile, but the purr of the truck and the smooth ride calmed him. Blue was resting in the back of the truck once again and seemed pleased with his heroic actions. Caleb had resumed his position in the cab and stared out the window. Jerry surveyed the scene and wondered what lay ahead of him in Washburn.

9

Jerry throttled the motor to conform to the lower speed limit as he approached the city limits of the tiny town of Washburn. He pulled the truck over to the ditch in front of the Mom and Pop store that had been at the intersection as long as he could remember. His heart raced when he recognized Highway 26, a county black top he and his brothers had spent many hours on, riding their bikes and playing. He clearly remembered when he was six years old the road was paved and he and Dale had decided they wanted to become truck drivers after watching the dump trucks bring their loads of asphalt. He was not sure he wanted to travel the three miles down Highway 26 to where he grew up at Last Stop. It was possible the place no longer existed. Though it was not quite dark, Caleb could awake at any moment and he would certainly be upset if Jerry was not where he was supposed to be. He looked back at Blue and saw he was asleep too, and he decided he was going to take a chance and find his old home place.

He accelerated the F100 and turned right onto the familiar road. The scenery had not changed much. There was pasture and pine trees along both sides of the road much as it was when Jerry was little. He noticed a few mobile homes dotted the country side, a sight that was not part of the landscape in the 60s. One other addition to the area was a saw mill situated about a quarter of a mile off the road near an old cypress pond. Just down the

101

road Jerry looked to his left and saw the graded road that he and Charlie used to ride down to buy Charlie's whiskey.

He passed another farmhouse and two more mobile homes until he reached the place he was looking for. On the left side of the road, where another county road intersected with Highway 26, Jerry saw it. He took a deep breath and put on the turn signal and made a left onto the property that Charlie Watson had owned and operated. He opened the driver's side door and got out of the truck. Blue jumped up and playfully licked Jerry's ear.

"Come on Blue." Jerry reached back and invited him to join him while he walked around the property. The metal pole that held the Last Stop sign, rusted and weather beaten indicated the place had changed names several times. Faded and dirty the barely visible words read, "Fred's Place." A touch of sadness filled Jerry when he viewed the rest of the property which had suffered a similar fate. Although his early years were not happy, he loved his mother and brothers and the place of his early childhood going to waste was difficult. The windows were broken, the screen on the double doors was brown and brittle; and Lettie's beautiful flower garden was undefined and overgrown.

When he stepped into the building, the memories he experienced that morning at the country store surged through him again. He could see the juke box; the car seat he used to hide behind; the bar stools the patrons would sit on; and the old Coca Cola box where his mother would give him a cool drink. There were huge holes in the wall and ceiling, weeds shot up through holes in the floor, and a scrawny rat was scurrying in the back of the room. Jerry, lost in thought, took a step forward and unexpectedly fell through a soft spot in the unstable floor. He tumbled toward a large drink box and thrust his hand out just in time to glance off it. Another inch and his head would have hit directly on the rusty jagged edge.

"Oh my! That was a close call." Jerry tried to wiggle himself out.

"Mr. Jerry!" The familiar sound of Caleb's voice filled the air. "You should not be here. Don't you see that you are being hindered from making your appointed destiny?"

By now Jerry had pulled himself up, viewed the damage to himself and brushed himself off. "What destiny? You said we must get to Washburn by dark and we made it. We're here! What more do you want?"

"No! No! No!" He shouted. "We must go to the nursing home and see Mrs. Richardson. That is your purpose for coming here. Don't you understand she holds the key to your peace and success? Come now, we must hurry."

By now Jerry had learned not to argue with Caleb. His purpose in going to Washburn was to see Mrs. Richardson, that much was true. He dutifully followed Caleb to the truck and whistled for Blue. Once they were all in the truck Jerry started the engine, but sat for just a moment and turned to Caleb and said. "This is where I lived as a kid."

"I know Mr. Jerry." Caleb said. "And I am sure it is difficult for you to see it in such condition. I don't wish to detract from your reflections on the past. But I must insist that we go immediately to Haven of Rest Nursing Home."

Jerry made his way back to the main intersection of Washburn and headed west. They passed several businesses he recognized.

"Look!" Jerry pointed to a place called Rachel's Restaurant. "That used to be Jeff's Texaco. That is where I spent many hours pumping gas. And over there is the church where my mama used to take us to Vacation Bible school in the summer." The truck crept along. "Up there on the hill is Washburn Elementary," Jerry pointed to a red brick building on his left. "That's where I met Mrs. Richardson." And then Jerry's countenance changed. He slowed the vehicle further when he crossed a railroad track. "That's where Fred Beasley was killed on that awful night so many years ago."

"I'm sorry." Caleb extended his hand and touched Jerry's shoulder.

"The nursing home is just around the corner." He changed the conversation and made a left and headed down a narrow paved street lined with willow trees.

After traveling about one hundred yards Jerry came to a stop behind several vehicles. "What is going on up there?" Jerry poked his head out the window to get a better view of why the traffic had suddenly stopped. "Oh! It's only a driver's license checkpoint. I haven't been in one of these in quite awhile."

"Mr. Jerry!" Caleb began in that tone of his. "Is there a way we can get around this checkpoint?"

"Why? I have my license and the truck is in tip top condition. This should be a snap."

"I do not think so. This minor traffic check will keep you from reaching the nursing home by dark." Caleb looked up through the windshield and saw the sun slowly setting, his breath quickened. "We must turn around and go another way."

"Hold on! You may have been right about other things, but this is not a problem."

"You do not have your wallet." Caleb said

dryly. "Not only that, you do not have a tag."

"Of course I have my wallet. It is right here." Jerry reached for his wallet in his hip pocket. "What! What did you do with it?"

"I have not taken your wallet." Caleb drew closer to him. "It was dislodged from your person when you scuffled with the stranger at the Texaco Station. I saw him pick it up just before he ran away."

"Why didn't you tell me?" Jerry complained and noticed the vehicles ahead of him were slowly moving forward.

"It would have done no good." Caleb sighed. "I also saw your tag was missing when you picked me up this morning. It must have been stolen or the screws came loose and you lost it. It really doesn't matter. All that matters is that you will be detained for some time if you go through that checkpoint."

Jerry stared blankly at the man for several seconds and then pressed the accelerator and whipped around the car in front of him. "I can take this side road and still get to the nursing home from here," he said.

In just a few minutes, after some maneuvering on Jerry's part, the truck was parked in front of the Haven of Rest Nursing Home. The sun was going down over the top of a China Berry tree located in the front yard of the long block building which housed the elderly patients. Paint was peeling from the eves of the building.

"This is it! Doesn't look much different than it did back in the 60s." Jerry leaned his head on the back window and thought out loud. "Mrs. Richardson deserves better."

"I encourage you to go in as quickly as possible. I'll stay out here with Blue while you go in and talk with your dear Mrs. Richardson." Caleb pushed the passenger door closed and invited the big dog to jump out of the truck with a whistle. They made their way to a small park adjacent to the building and Jerry walked onto the front porch of the nursing home. He opened the glass door and stepped into a large room with several chairs and a couple of sofas against the wall. To the right was a receptionist's desk which was empty. He made his way to the desk and started to ring the bell when he noticed a handwritten note on a legal pad which read, *Need new crank on bed-Richardson Rm 28.*

"Richardson? That's got to be her room." Jerry's pulse quickened. He located rooms 1 through 32 by an arrow pointing to a long hallway. He looked around for an attendant but did not see anyone and decided he would visit her without asking. It was strangely quiet on the wing. The freshly mopped floors smelled antiseptic. On his way to her room he tried to remember Mrs. Richardson as she was, standing before her class in her white blouse, blue skirt, navy high heels and - gold necklace. He was anxious to see if she recognized him.

The door to room 28 was partially open. Jerry tapped lightly with his bare knuckles and called, "Hello?"

"Yes," an older female voice returned. "Come in."

The voice was a bit softer and weaker, but Jerry recognized it as that of Mrs. Richardson. It still carried the love and compassion Jerry remembered so well. He slowly pushed open the door and stepped into the dimly lit room. Sitting in a wheelchair in the corner of the room next to a hospital bed was Mrs. Richardson. Her hair was white, she seemed somewhat smaller, but it was unmistakably she. Jerry drew in a deep breath. "Mrs. Richardson?" he called gently.

"Yes! Who is there? I"m afraid I can't see as well as I used to."

Jerry moved closer. "Mrs. Richardson. It's Jerry, Jerry Watson. Do you remember me?"

"Jerry!" Mrs. Richardson's eyes brightened and a broad smile covered her face. She reached her hands out toward him. "My boy. Come here and let me hold you."

Jerry leaned forward and the elderly woman tenderly cupped his face with her hands and kissed him on his forehead. She studied him for a moment. "Oh, Jerry, I love you so much." And she pulled him to her once again.

Jerry's eyes welled up with tears. His thoughts took him to that day he left Mrs. Richardson's class for the last time. He had hugged her, then burst into tears.

After several moments he pulled away and looked her in the face. Her hair, though white with age, was perfectly in place. She had on make up and lipstick livened her lips. She was wearing a beautiful red blouse and black pants, her favorite colors, and a wool blanket covered her legs.

"Master Jerry Watson, sit here." She motioned to a plastic chair beside her. As he settled in she asked, "What are you doing in little Washburn. I was worried that you might not remember us now that you work for the President."

"Mrs. Richardson, I could never forget you." Jerry looked down. "But I must ask you to forgive me for not staying in touch with you more. I am not sure why I am here. I felt like I needed to see you. Things are not going very well for me at the moment. Maybe there is something that I need to reconstruct, or reinforce, or something.

"Jerry, do you remember the last day of school when I hugged you and you burst into tears?"

"Yes ma'am. I could never forget that day. It was a turning point in my life."

"I asked you what you wanted to do with your life and you told me you wanted to be a lawyer," she continued. "Do you remember?"

"Yes. I said I wanted to help people. And you took me down to the basement and showed me The Creed. Did you know that I still have the certificate you gave me. I read it often."

"Jerry, I knew that you could do it, that you would employ these principles in your life and become a success. And though you got off track in your teenage years you finally settled down and became the person I knew you could be."

"But I don't feel like a success. I know I have employed these principles but something seems to be missing."

"Jerry, as you will recall, there are four principles in The Creed." Then she reached over to the other side of her chair and Jerry let out a gasp. It looked like the trunk she used to keep in the basement. "You are right. It is the trunk I kept for many years in the basement at Washburn Elementary. Can you help me get the little book?"

Jerry went to the trunk and retrieved the little brown book that Mrs. Richardson had read from when he was in sixth grade. He handed it to her and she opened it to a place she had marked with a faded red ribbon. "As you know the fourth principle is Take Personal Responsibility for Your Actions."

"And I have done that, to a fault. I am willing to take the blame even where it is not clear whose fault it is. I am a very responsible person."

"I think that is quite clear by the fact the President has put such faith in you. And of course you took responsibility for the crime you committed and served your time. Now, the third principle is Hard Work. I am amazed at the young people today who think that somebody owes them something. It is still hard work that makes you a success. I am sure you are a hard worker, or you wouldn't be where you are today."

"You said a mouthful there Mrs. Richardson. My wife Mary Ann calls me a workaholic. I take great pride in my work ethic and my work product. There are times that I compete with people who are smarter than I, but I out work them."

"The second principle is Get an Education. Jerry, I am so proud of you. Although you quit school in the tenth grade, you saw the importance of an education and went back to school. A law degree from Duke University is a great achievement my boy."

"I realized that with a good education I could attain my wildest dreams."

"You surely did.

"Jerry, it is obvious that the virtues of The Creed are working in your life."

Jerry lowered his head again and shook it slowly. "If that is true, then why am I so unhappy? Why do I feel like such a failure? How could my life fall apart if The Creed is working?"

"My, my. You are troubled my son. There is one fundamental we have not talked about, and quite frankly, it is the most important one–Faith in God. Jerry, have you placed your trust in God."

"I believe in God, I go to church with Mary Ann and the kids when I get a chance. She is always praying for me. I am not a bad person."

"But have you placed your trust in God

through Jesus Christ?"

"Well, I think Jesus was a good person with good teachings. I try and live by what He taught."

"Oh! my boy. Don't you understand? It is not how much you try to be a good person. You must trust in Jesus with your whole heart. Your problem is that you do not have a relationship with Him. You must understand that you are a sinner, incapable of saving yourself. You need a Savior."

"I've never really thought about Jesus in terms of a personal relationship. I thought all you had to do was believe in God. That there are lots of ways to Him."

"Hand me that Bible, please." Mrs. Richardson pointed to a small table near her bed. "Jesus said, I am the way, the truth, and life. No man cometh unto the Father but by me."

For several minutes she expounded scripture that Jerry had heard preachers share in church. Suddenly it was as if a light went off and the heavens opened. It was an incredible spiritual experience. All at once it hit him. He realized what was missing. All those times Mary Ann and the kids talked about their relationship with Jesus. He just could not see it, but now, he finally understood. He could not explain it, but it was like it all came together in a flash. What he needed was a relationship. He had been trusting in religion.

"Mrs. Richardson?"

"Yes son."

"Can you tell me what I must do to be saved?"

"Jerry, pray this prayer with me." She took his hand and prayed. "Lord, I am a sinner and I cannot save myself. I believe that Jesus Christ came to earth, died, was buried and rose again. I believe His blood is the only thing that can cleanse me from my sin. I accept you into my life as my Lord and Savior."

Jerry sincerely repeated the prayer.

"Now let me pray for you son." Jerry lay his head on her bosom and she prayed. "Lord, thank you for my brother in the Lord and son in the faith. Help him to live for you from this day forward. Help him do his job faithfully. Protect him from those who want to harm him. Amen."

Jerry burst into tears and sobbed uncontrollably as he did on the last day of school. She consoled him and patted his head. "It's okay son. I love you, and Jesus loves you."

"How could I have been so blind all these years?" Jerry lifted his face and looked into her beautiful eyes. "The answer was right before me all along. You don't know how much weight has been lifted from me."

"I think I understand it." Then she looked longingly out the window at the fading sunset and said. "You must go now, I have something I must attend to." She bent forward once more and kissed his face. "I love you Master Jerry Watson."

"I love you, Mrs. Richardson." He wiped the tears from his eyes and stood to his feet. "I'll be back to see you, and I'll bring Mary Ann with me."

"I'll see you on the other side," she said simply and waved her hand.

Jerry turned and left her presence a new man. He skipped his way out of the room and down the hall. He thought it odd that he never saw one other person in the building. When he reached the truck, Caleb and Blue were anxiously waiting for him. He opened the driver's side and jumped in, a wide smile on his lips.

"What happened in there?" Caleb wanted to know.

10

"That's an amazing story Mr. Jerry." Caleb seemed more relaxed than he had been since Jerry had picked him up that morning. He was almost jovial. He leaned back in his seat and enjoyed the ride north on Interstate 75.

"Something happened to me back there and I want to tell everybody about it, especially Mary Ann. I can't wait until I get home tonight."

"So, you are going home, are you?"

"I am, Caleb." Jerry gripped the steering wheel with both hands and hunched over it. "There is something I must face when I reach Atlanta, but I feel a tremendous burden has been lifted from me." Jerry swallowed a lump and looked into the distance. "I have a story to tell."

"Indeed you do, Mr. Jerry."

Jerry looked over at Caleb and asked rather sheepishly. "Are you a religious man?"

"I guess you might say that." Caleb chuckled.

"Caleb," he began, "everything seemed so strange this morning.113 But now that these extraordinary events have taken place, I believe that you were somehow directed to help me, that our paths crossed on purpose. What do you think about that?"

A soft smile curled his lips. "I know the Lord works in mysterious ways. If I have somehow been of service to you today, in helping you discover a truth that has assisted you, then, yes, I would say we were brought together."

"Caleb, I have a lot of questions I would like to ask you."

"I know you do, Mr. Jerry." Caleb turned toward him and gazed at him with those big beautiful eyes. "Like, Who am I? Where did I come from? How did I know you needed to go to Washburn? Are these some of your questions?"

"Well, it seems you have a pretty good understanding of things."

"But I think it best that we leave it alone for now." And he slid down in his seat, leaned his head back and closed his eyes. In a few moments he was snoring.

Jerry checked the approaching sign announcing Macon, Georgia was forty miles ahead. He reflected on the day's events. He was a changed man. He no longer cared about the prestige of his position. God and his family were the most important aspect of his life. He no longer feared others would find out about his past. He had no past. His future was now exciting.

Jerry had made up his mind that he was going back to Atlanta and face the reporters. If he was fired by the president, then that was okay with him. Actually it would be a relief. He still had his family, and now he had the Lord. He thought about moving to a smaller city and opening up a law office. He always wanted to help people. That is why he went to law school. He checked his watch. It was 9:30 p.m. He calculated they would make one more stop for something to eat before they reached Atlanta at about midnight. He reached over and opened the truck pocket to see if he had a few bucks stashed away, which he did. His thoughts drifted toward Mary Ann and home. For the first time he reached for the phone to make a call.

He dialed the number that was so familiar to

him. He pressed the send button and in seconds he heard it ringing. There was a click on the other end and the sweet, gentle voice of Mary Ann Watson came on the line. "Hello." It seemed it had been a life time since he had heard that voice.

"Hello, Honey."

"Jerry! Is it really you? I thought you were *in cognito* for a few days. I'm holding down the fort here and telling everybody I don't know where you are. By the way, where are you?"

"I'm on I-75 just south of Macon. Caleb, Blue and I are going to stop for a snack and then we're heading home."

"Caleb? Who's Caleb?"

"It is a long story. He is somebody I picked up this morning. Mary Ann, he is a very unique person. I can't wait for you to meet him."

"Sounds, exciting. So how's Blue?"

"He's great. I'm anxious to tell you what happened to me today. Mary Ann, you won't believe it."

"Jerry, you sound different. Something must have happened. Tell me now."

"I can't now. I don't want to talk about it over the phone. I want to see your beautiful face when I tell you. We'll be home in a couple of hours. Have the guest room ready for Caleb. I love you."

"I love you too, Hon. Bye bye."

Jerry enjoyed driving in the cool evenings. Though normally busy, I-75 seemed to be relatively calm on this cool spring evening, at least in the north bound lane. Jerry appreciated the by-pass around Macon and decided to take it. Soon he spotted a sign for gas and food and maneuvered to the right lane.

He reached over and tugged at Caleb's sleeve.

"Caleb? Wake up."

"Wha... What?"

"We are stopping for a little something to eat." Jerry motored onto the exit ramp and stopped at the end. He turned right and headed for a Shell station that offered food and refreshments. He pulled to the side of the building and announced, "I am going to the rest room, and then I am going to get Blue some water and something to eat. He looks like he is ready to eat a horse. I'll get us something also. What do you want?"

"I do not require any refreshment Mr. Jerry. But you go right ahead. I think I will get out and stretch my legs."

Jerry visited the restroom and then went in the store and purchased two sandwiches, a drink and bottle of water. When he returned to the truck Caleb was standing beside it with his back pack in his hand.

"What are you doing with that?" he asked him.

"It is time for me to go my way, Mr. Jerry." The stranger whose demeanor had changed so many times that day seemed old again, his voice soft and sad.

"I thought you said you were going west. How can you go west from here? You must let me take you to Atlanta and meet my wife, Mary Ann, then you can go."

"I would love to meet her, and I am sure I will one day. But there has been a change in my plans and I must head south again."

"South? But Caleb...."

"Do not ask me to stay, nor ask me why. Just trust that our meeting was appointed and that we will meet again." The old man walked over to him and opened his arms wide. The two embraced in a

116

long and emotional hug. Then Jerry and Blue watched as Caleb turned away and walked toward the south bound ramp.

"But how will you get to your destination?"

"The same way I got here." Caleb called back and gave a wave of the hand. "Good bye Mr. Jerry, and thank you for a splendid day. Good bye Blue."

"Good bye, Caleb, and God bless you."

Blue barked his salutation and Caleb made his way under the bright lights of the gas island. Jerry reached down to pat Blue on the head, "Blue, that is an extraordinary man." Then he remembered that he did not get an address or telephone number. When he looked up Caleb was gone. There were no cars in sight. "Where did he go?" Blue yapped a response.

"Get in Blue." Jerry grabbed his collar and helped him in the back of the truck. He dashed around to the driver's side and started the engine, wheeled around to the front of the station and headed for the south bound entrance ramp. There was no trace of Caleb, nor of anyone or any vehicle. Jerry whipped the truck around and headed back to the station and went past it a ways. Again he saw no one. "Where did he go?" Jerry turned and swerved into the station, stopped in front of the store and got out of the truck. He ran over to a teenage boy who was pumping gas. An older woman with kids in the car was next to him. "Did you see the old man that was with me tonight?"

"What old man?" the boy asked.

"The man that was with me over there just a few minutes ago." Jerry pointed in the direction where Caleb left him and Blue. "He left walking in the direction of the Interstate."

"I didn't see no old man, Sir."

"How about you ma'am?"

117

"I didn't see anyone either," she said rather nervously.

Jerry then rushed into the store where the attendant was behind the counter serving a man. A young lady was in the back buying a gallon of milk. "Did any of you see an old man, wearing blue jeans, a western shirt, and tennis shoes?"

The three persons turned and looked at Jerry. "I asked, Did any of you see an old gentleman come in here in the last two or three minutes?"

"There hasn't been an old man in here in the last hour," the attendant said.

"I ain't seen nobody like that in here," the man responded.

The woman turned back to her milk and did not say anything to Jerry. He raced back to the truck and Blue. "He's got to be here somewhere. Somebody must have seen him." He started the engine and spun out of the parking lot and toward the south bound lane once again and entered it. He zoomed down the Interstate in the direction from which he had just come. However, there was no one in sight, just the constant flow of traffic heading south. He slowed down and pulled off into the emergency lane and stopped. He rolled down his window and hollered, "Caleb, where are you?" Blue yelped once again. ...

At 6:30 Friday morning the silver Mercedes pulled onto Willow Lane. It had been a short night for Jerry and Mary Ann. They had stayed up until 3:30 talking about his experiences at the old store, with Mrs. Richardson, and Caleb. Mary Ann was thrilled that he had made a commitment to serve the Lord and she was so gracious in receiving the news about his past. She also agreed that the information should not be concealed and assured him of her support. When they finally went to bed he could not sleep. Caleb and his strange disappearance kept going through his mind. He was reluctant to talk about the experience. It seemed so sacred. And when Mary Ann tried to make a connection between Caleb and his spiritual experience, he changed the subject.

It was still early and Jerry avoided much of the rush hour traffic. He pulled the sleek Mercedes into the parking garage and stopped at the security window. "Good morning, Mr. Watson." Ernie Stranch had been the parking lot attendant for as long as Jerry could remember.

"Good morning, Ernie." Jerry waved and flashed his identification card just as he had done every morning for the past fifteen years. As he pulled through the gate, Ernie called out. "By the way, that news team is already here."

Jerry stopped the car. "What news team?"

"The team from the CNN Center. They said you knew they would be here so I let them in." Ernie gave a wave and Jerry drove into the parking garage.

"Thank you, Lord," Jerry breathed out his anxiety. "I know what I have to do, I know it is right, and with God's help I am going to do it."

The elevator ride up to the 40th floor was the fastest Jerry could remember. He was alone in the private elevator, as often was the case, since he arrived so early to work each morning. The door finally opened in the rear of the offices and Jerry headed toward his private entrance. Before he could reach the door he was met by the floor security guard.

"Mr. Watson!" Steve called out. "There's a crew of reporters in the reception room. They said they are here to see you and that you know it. I told them there's no way you would schedule a meeting this early in the morning. I don't know how they got past Ernie and security downstairs. I don't trust them media types."

How did they get past security? Jerry thought. And though they had lied, he did know they were coming. He could have called the police and had the intruders removed from the building, but he would not do that. He was not worried about what was going to take place. He had a peace about it all and believed that everything was going to be all right.

"Steve, I appreciate your concern. You are doing a great job looking out for me and the firm. But I am expecting these people and I am looking forward to meeting with them. Would you tell them that I will be with them in about thirty minutes."

"Uh, yes Sir."

"And Steve?"

"Yes, Mr. Watson?"

"Ask them if they would like a cup of coffee while they are waiting." Jerry smiled and turned the key to his door.

"Uh, yes Sir." Steve looked puzzled as he walked toward the reception area.

At precisely 8:01 a. m. Mrs. Reed called Jerry over the intercom. "Mr. Watson! There is a full camera crew from CNN sitting in the reception area drinking coffee. They insist that they have an appointment with you, but you're not supposed to be here. And I don't believe them for a moment," she exclaimed. "By the way, what are you doing here?"

"I'm back for the battle," Jerry chuckled. "And don't worry about those reporters. They are invited guests."

"Yes Sir."

"And, Mrs. Reed, do you believe in miracles?"

"What?! I mean, I guess I do. Why do you ask?"

"Because I experienced a miraculous change yesterday. I can't wait to tell you about it. And I will, but not right now. First, I have some unfinished business to take care of. Send in the reporters. I am ready to see them now." Jerry stood to his full six feet and faced the dreaded moment with a certain lightheartedness that was unexplainable. When Adrian Phillips stepped into his office Jerry eagerly reached out with his hand and welcomed him to his office. ...

Jerry flipped off the television and returned to his position on the couch beside Mary Ann. "Focus on People," the human interest program on CNN which aired every Friday night at 7:00 p. m. had just ended.

"I can't believe I told them the whole story Mary Ann. I caught them by surprise. When Adrian Phillips finally got around to asking me about my past I held nothing back, he was incredulous," Jerry gleefully stated. He looked at his wife of twenty seven years and stroked her hair. "I am just sorry I never told you."

"Oh Jerry. I told you last night that all that matters is that you got things right with the Lord. You did what you thought was best for us. You know I forgive you." She leaned her head on his shoulder.

"I phoned the White House and warned Nicole about the interview. I wanted them to be prepared for the questions that will obviously come their way." He bent over and kissed her head. "I do not want to bring reproach upon the President, but I know I can't live a lie any longer. I'm prepared to take my licks, even if it means being fired. Do you think you could live with a country lawyer representing clients who can pay only with a few eggs, a side of bacon, or basket of corn?"

"Jerry, let me remind you that you weren't that important when we met that day on the intramural field. Do you remember?"

"How could I forget? I nearly killed you with that errant pass before I had a chance to get to know you, much less marry you." They both laughed.

"Honey, I can tell the change in you. I have always loved you, but there is something new about you that makes me love you more, if that is possible."

Jerry reached over and removed the phone from the hook and he and Mary Ann spent the next hour reminiscing about their lives together, from that chance meeting at Duke University through the years of building a successful law practice and having children, and then being thrust into the spotlight as an advisor to the President of the United States. The stillness of the evening was broken by the ring of the special phone the White House had installed in Jerry's home office so the President could reach him at any time. The two of them looked at each other for what seemed like an eternity. Finally Jerry got up and walked to the roll top desk in the corner of the room.

"That will be Nicole. Pray for me, this is it." He picked up the phone. "Hello."

Jerry paused while the other party spoke. Nicole Jantzen was the President's Chief of Staff and was the one who usually called Jerry. In less important matters she would convey the President's wishes and Jerry would execute them.

"Yes, Nicole. I understand. I'll hold." Mary Ann scanned Jerry's expressionless face for some indication of what was transpiring on the other end of the line.

He was standing tall and straight, a picture of the proud man that he was. "Hello Mr. President." Mary Ann's mouth fell open. "Sir, I am sure you are calling about the CNN report, and let me just say that I understand what you must do." Jerry braced himself.

As the conversation continued, Mary Ann could see that Jerry relaxed more and a smile pursed his lips. She was puzzled by his reaction to the President's words. He was nodding and agreeing with the man on the other line. After a very long time, Jerry hung up the phone and looked at Mary Ann with a silly grin on his face.

"What's going on?" she burst out.

"You won't believe it!"

"What?" She jumped up and ran to him. "What did the President of the United States tell you?"

"Mary Ann! You just won't believe what President Morton said." He slid down in a leather chair beside the desk. The grin changed to a look of bewilderment. "I expected at least a rebuke from Nicole, and, at worst, a firing. But it is incredible what just took place."

"Well tell me about it. I can't stand it anymore."

"Sit here beside me." Jerry took her hand and guided her to a seat beside him. "Mary Ann, the President thanked me for being open and honest. He said that my performance on the program reminded him of the reason he went into politics to begin with. He wanted to provide an alternative to the dishonesty that is so prevalent in government. He said that he had underestimated the stress and pressure he would be under as President of the United States and that he had gotten away from some of the basic values that he held so dear."

"You know that he is a Christian."

"Yes, he reminded me of that. He said that my openness in sharing my testimony about what the Lord did for me helped him. He wants men like me in his camp because I represent decency and honesty. He believes that my presentation will help restore trust and confidence in our government. He is behind me no matter what the pollsters make of this."

"Oh, Jerry I am so thrilled." Mary Ann hugged him.

"One more thing Mary Ann. He said he and Mrs. Morton watched the interview together and when it was over he wept. He said he came under conviction because he felt he had compromised some of his beliefs when he allowed the pressures of his office to cause him to detour from those beliefs. They both kneeled down in the family quarters of the White House and prayed and asked God to help them be godly leaders for this country."

"Jerry, it is overwhelming to see how you influenced the most powerful man in the world."

Jerry leaned his head back and mused for a moment. "Divine. It has been a divine week. I wish Caleb were here to share in this with me. I hope somehow he got a chance to see the program." Jerry leaped to his feet. "Wait a minute!"

"What!?"

"Mrs. Richardson! I forgot about Mrs. Richardson. She's the one who really deserves the credit. I've got to call her." He ran over and sat on the edge of the couch and reached for the phone.

He dialed information, received the number for Haven of Rest Nursing Home, dialed it, and after several rings a woman's voice came on the other line. "Good evening, Haven of Rest, how may I direct your call?"

"Hello, this is Jerry Watson. I would like to speak with Mrs. Richardson. She should be in Room 28."

"Are you a relative sir?"

"No I am just a good friend, as a matter of fact I was one of her students in sixth grade many years ago."

"I understand sir, but I cannot release information to you if you are not a relative."

"What kind of information? I just want to talk with her."

"I am sorry but I cannot give you any details. You will have to contact the family."

"What are you talking about?"

"One moment please." The line went flat and Jerry held the phone to his ear and gave Mary Ann a shrug.

"Hello, this is Supervisor Hayes, may I help you?"

"Hi, this is Jerry Watson in Atlanta. I was calling to speak with Mrs. Richardson."

"Oh, yes, Mr. Watson." The voice lightened up. "I feel like I know you though I have never met you. You see I am one of the nurses who has written you on Mrs. Richardson's behalf. I want you to know we really appreciate all that you did for her."

"Thank you. But what I did was only a small repayment for what she did for me. Is it possible to speak with her?"

The woman's tone changed. "I am so sorry Mr. Watson, but Mrs. Richardson died last evening."

"What!" Jerry's face turned ashen, he lowered the phone and turned to his wife.

"What is it, Honey?" she asked anxiously.

"Mrs. Richardson. She died last night."

Jerry raised the phone to his ear and asked, "What happened?"

"She had not been well for quite some time, Mr. Watson. And then of course she was in her eighties."

"What time did she die?"

"I don't know exactly, but it was just about dark when she passed away. I had just finished writing my reports when I felt like I needed to check on her. When I entered the room she leaned back in her chair and mumbled something. It sounded like she said, 'I can go home now.' And then she closed her eyes. It was the most peaceful home going I have ever seen. And I have seen quite a few here over the years."

"Mrs. Hayes, I was there at Haven of Rest yesterday afternoon and visited Mrs. Richardson. She seemed to be in good health. I'm shocked."

"Oh really? You must have seen her just before she died. I am sorry I missed you. There was something very strange about the whole thing."

"What was that?"

"It was very odd that she spoke so coherently," the nurse explained.

"What do you mean by that?"

"Well, as I am sure you discovered, not many people knew about her condition. The nurses did her correspondence for the last few years because Mrs. Richardson had a continuing bout with Alzheimer's disease. It degenerated to the extent that she was noncommunicative for the last two years."

"What! What do you mean she didn't communicate for the last two years? I talked with her yesterday."

"I am sure you talked with her, Mr. Watson, but I am quite sure she did not talk with you, not where you could understand her anyway."

"I tell you I talked with her and she talked with me. We had an intelligent conversation and I understood everything she said. She was coherent and in her right mind."

"Mr. Watson, I have taken care of Mrs. Richardson for the past five years, I have seen her every day. I watched as her family and loved ones tried to get her to respond to them, and she never did, not once. I am sure you are mistaken. Now you may call Croft Funeral Home and they will advise you about the arrangements. Thank you and good night."

Jerry dropped the receiver into its cradle and looked at Mary Ann.

"Honey! What was that all about?"

"I don't understand. The nurse said Mrs. Richardson could not have talked with me yesterday. She said she has had Alzheimer's for several years and has not talked with her own family for two years."

"What!!?? What does all of this mean?"

"I don't know, Honey." Jerry reached for Mary Ann and held her in his arms. "I don't know for sure, but I believe I understand why things happened the way they did this week." He looked heavenward and smiled.